APR 1 7 2018

# the GARFIELD show

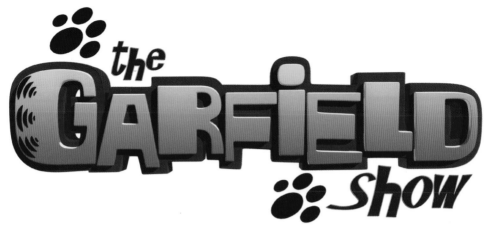

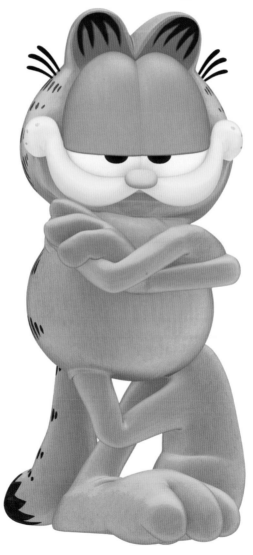

PAPERCUTZ™

# GARFIELD GRAPHIC NOVELS AVAILABLE FROM PAPERCUTZ™

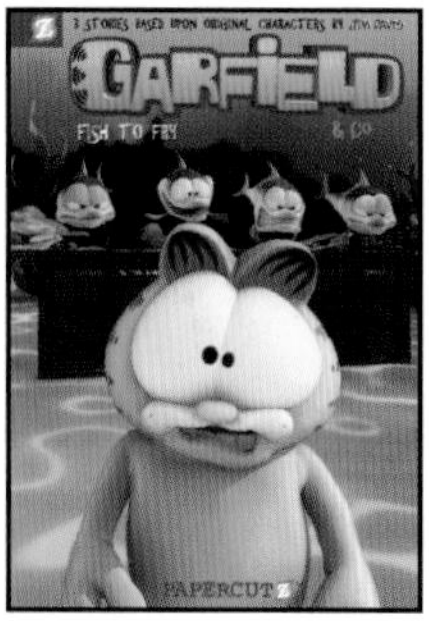
GARFIELD
& Co
FISH TO FRY
PAPERCUTZ

GARFIELD & Co #1
"FISH TO FRY"

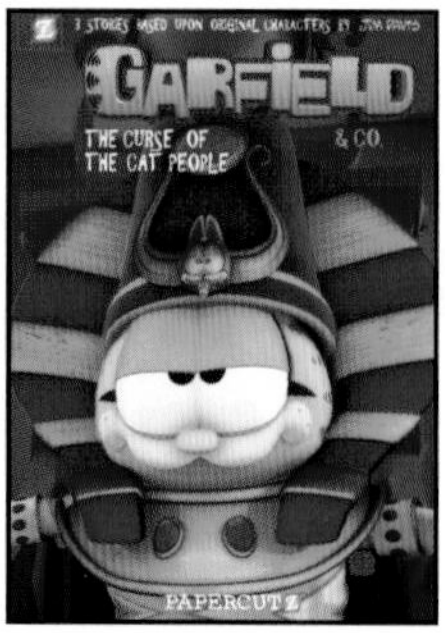
GARFIELD
& Co
THE CURSE OF THE CAT PEOPLE
PAPERCUTZ

GARFIELD & Co #2
"THE CURSE OF
THE CAT PEOPLE"

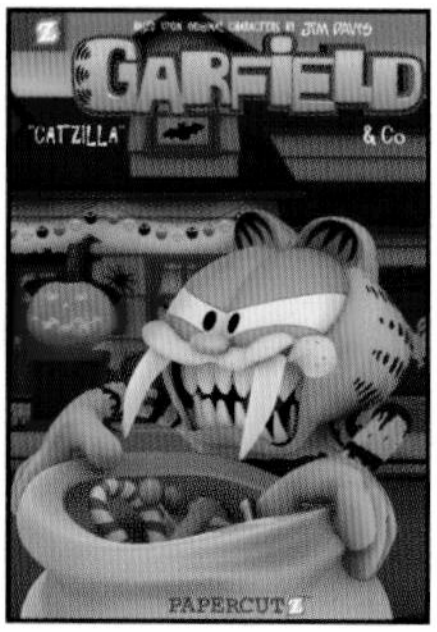
GARFIELD
& Co
"CATZILLA"
PAPERCUTZ

GARFIELD & Co #3
"CATZILLA"

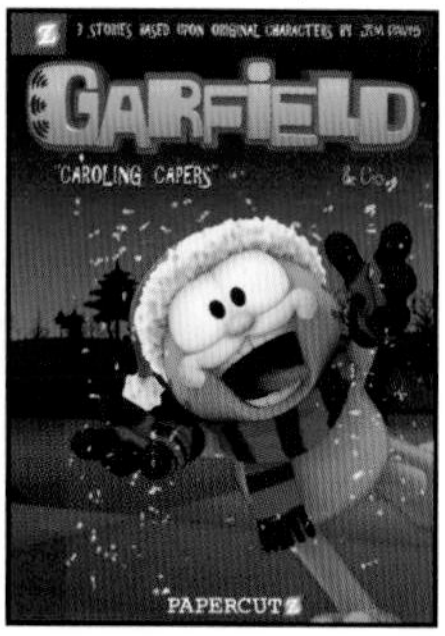
GARFIELD
& Co
"CAROLING CAPERS"
PAPERCUTZ

GARFIELD & Co #4
"CAROLING CAPERS"

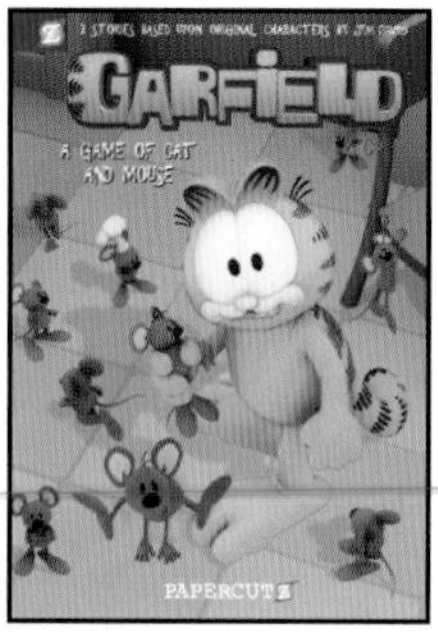
GARFIELD
A GAME OF CAT AND MOUSE
PAPERCUTZ

GARFIELD & Co #5
"A GAME OF CAT
AND MOUSE"

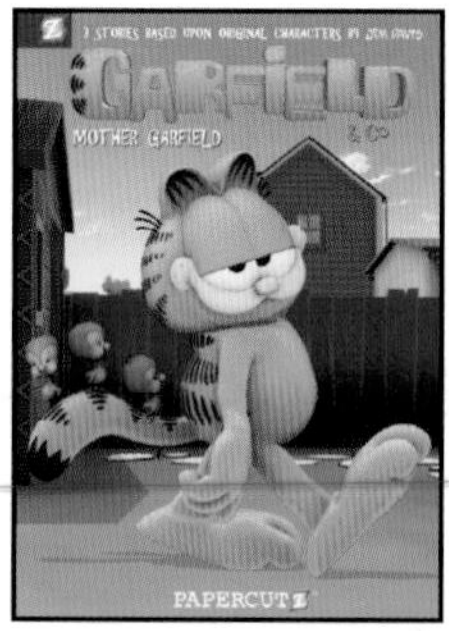
GARFIELD
& Co
MOTHER GARFIELD
PAPERCUTZ

GARFIELD & Co #6
"MOTHER GARFIELD"

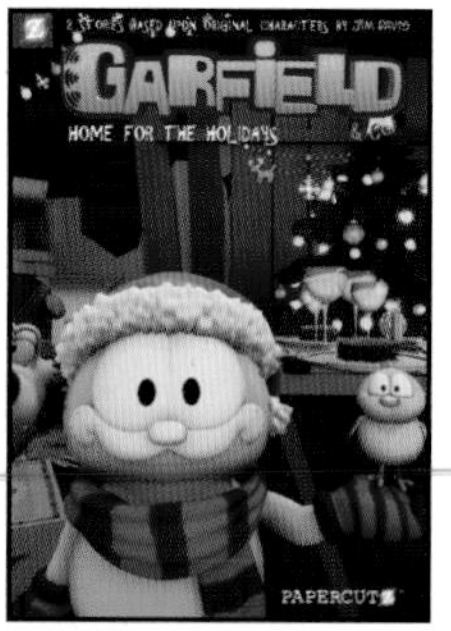
GARFIELD
& Co
HOME FOR THE HOLIDAYS
PAPERCUTZ

GARFIELD & Co #7
"HOME FOR THE
HOLIDAYS"

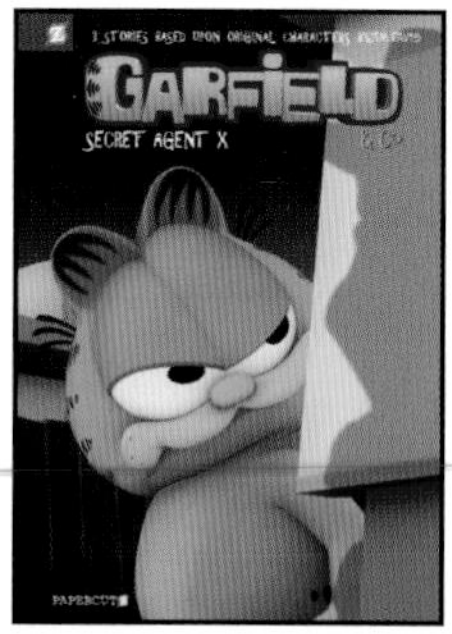
GARFIELD
& Co
SECRET AGENT X

GARFIELD & Co #8
"SECRET AGENT X"

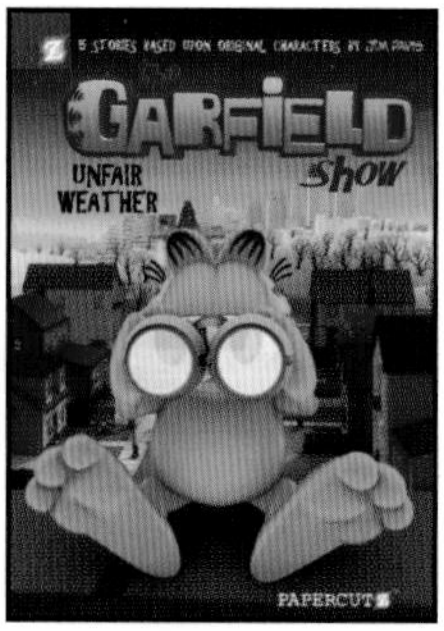
GARFIELD
show
UNFAIR WEATHER
PAPERCUTZ

THE GARFIELD SHOW #1
"UNFAIR WEATHER"

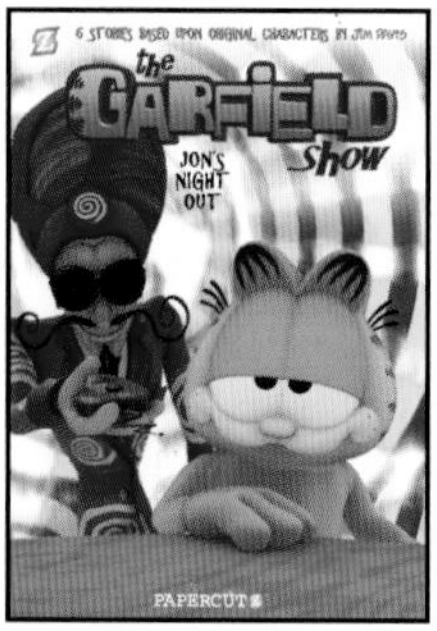
the GARFIELD show
JON'S NIGHT OUT
PAPERCUTZ

COMING SOON:
THE GARFIELD SHOW #2
"JON'S NIGHT OUT"

**GARFIELD & Co GRAPHIC NOVELS ARE AVAILABLE IN HARDCOVER ONLY FOR $7.99 EACH. THE GARFIELD SHOW GRAPHIC NOVELS ARE $7.99 IN PAPERBACK, AND $11.99 IN HARDCOVER. AVAILABLE FROM BOOKSELLERS EVERYWHERE..**

YOU CAN ALSO ORDER ONLINE FROM PAPERCUTZ.COM OR CALL 1-800-886-1223, MONDAY THROUGH FRIDAY, 9 - 5 EST. MC, VISA, AND AMEX ACCEPTED. TO ORDER BY MAIL, PLEASE ADD $4.00 FOR POSTAGE AND HANDLING FOR FIRST BOOK ORDERED, $1.00 FOR EACH ADDITIONAL BOOK, AND MAKE CHECK PAYABLE TO NBM PUBLISHING. SEND TO: PAPERCUTZ, 160 BROADWAY, SUITE 700, EAST WING, NEW YORK, NY 10038.

# the GARFIELD show

## #1 "UNFAIR WEATHER"

BASED ON THE ORIGINAL CHARACTERS CREATED BY

## JIM DAVIS

PAPERCUTZ ™

NEW YORK

THE GARFIELD SHOW #1 "UNFAIR WEATHER"

"THE GARFIELD SHOW" SERIES ℗ 2013- DARGAUD MEDIA. ALL RIGHTS RESERVED. ℗ PAWS. "GARFIELD" & GARFIELD CHARACTERS ™ & ℗ PAWS INC. - ALL RIGHTS RESERVED. THE GARFIELD SHOW—A DARGAUD MEDIA PRODUCTION. IN ASSO-CIATION WITH FRANCE3 WITH THE PARTICIPATION OF CENTRE NATIONAL DE LA CINÉMETOGRAPHIE AND THE SUPPORT OF REGION ILE-DE-FRANCE. A SERIES DE-VELOPED BY PHILIPPE VIDAL, ROBERT REA AND STEVE BALISSAT. BASED UPON THE CHARACTERS CREATED BY JIM DAVIS. ORIGINAL STORIES: "UNFAIR WEATH-ER" AND "WICKED WISHES" WRITTEN BY MARK EVANIER; "MAILMAN BLUES" WRIT-TEN BY PETER BERTS; "THE ROBOT" WRITTEN BY BAPTISTE HEIDRICH; "DOWN ON THE FARM" WRITTEN BY CHRISTOPHE POUJOL.

CEDRIC MICHIELS - COMICS ADAPTATION
JOE JOHNSON - TRANSLATIONS
JIM SALICRUP - DIALOGUE RESTORATION
JANICE CHIANG - LETTERING
BETH SCORZATO - PRODUCTION COORDINATOR
MICHAEL PETRANEK - EDITOR
JIM SALICRUP
EDITOR-IN-CHIEF


ISBN: 978-1-59707-422-3 PAPERBACK EDITION
ISBN: 978-1-59707-433-9 HARDCOVER EDITION

PRINTED IN CHINA
MAY 2013 BY O.G. PRINTING PRODUCTIONS, LTD.
UNITS 2 & 3, 5/F, LEMMI CENTRE
50 HOI YUEN ROAD
KWON TONG, KOWLOON

PAPERCUTZ BOOKS MAY BE PURCHASED FOR BUSINESS OR PROMOTIONAL USE. FOR INFORMATION ON BULK PURCHASES PLEASE CONTACT MACMILLAN CORPORATE AND PREMIUM SALES DEPARTMENT AT (800) 221-7945 X5442.


DISTRIBUTED BY MACMILLAN

FIRST PAPERCUTZ PRINTING

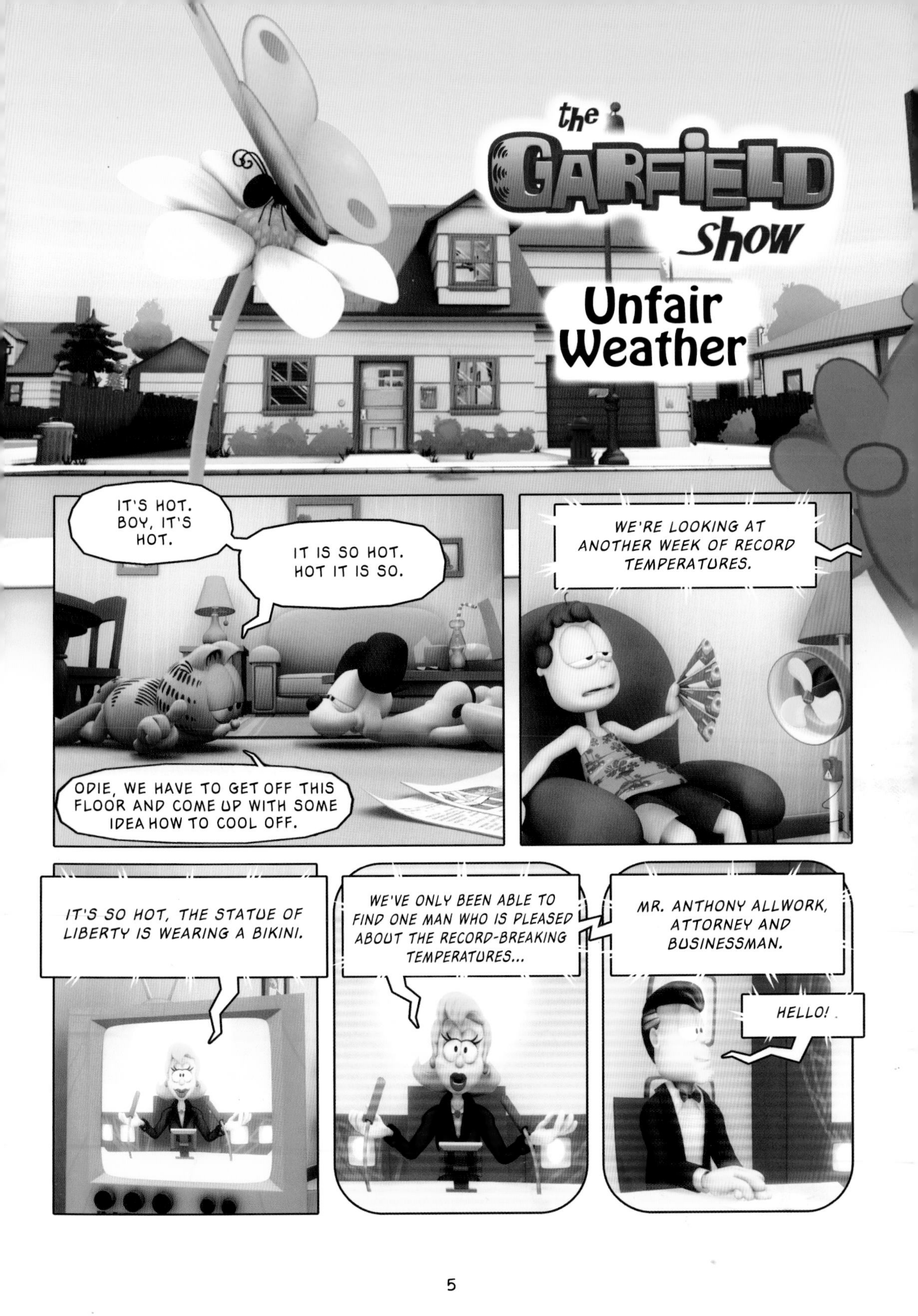
the GARFIELD show
Unfair Weather
IT'S HOT. BOY, IT'S HOT.
IT IS SO HOT. HOT IT IS SO.
ODIE, WE HAVE TO GET OFF THIS FLOOR AND COME UP WITH SOME IDEA HOW TO COOL OFF.
WE'RE LOOKING AT ANOTHER WEEK OF RECORD TEMPERATURES.
IT'S SO HOT, THE STATUE OF LIBERTY IS WEARING A BIKINI.
WE'VE ONLY BEEN ABLE TO FIND ONE MAN WHO IS PLEASED ABOUT THE RECORD-BREAKING TEMPERATURES...
MR. ANTHONY ALLWORK, ATTORNEY AND BUSINESSMAN.
HELLO!

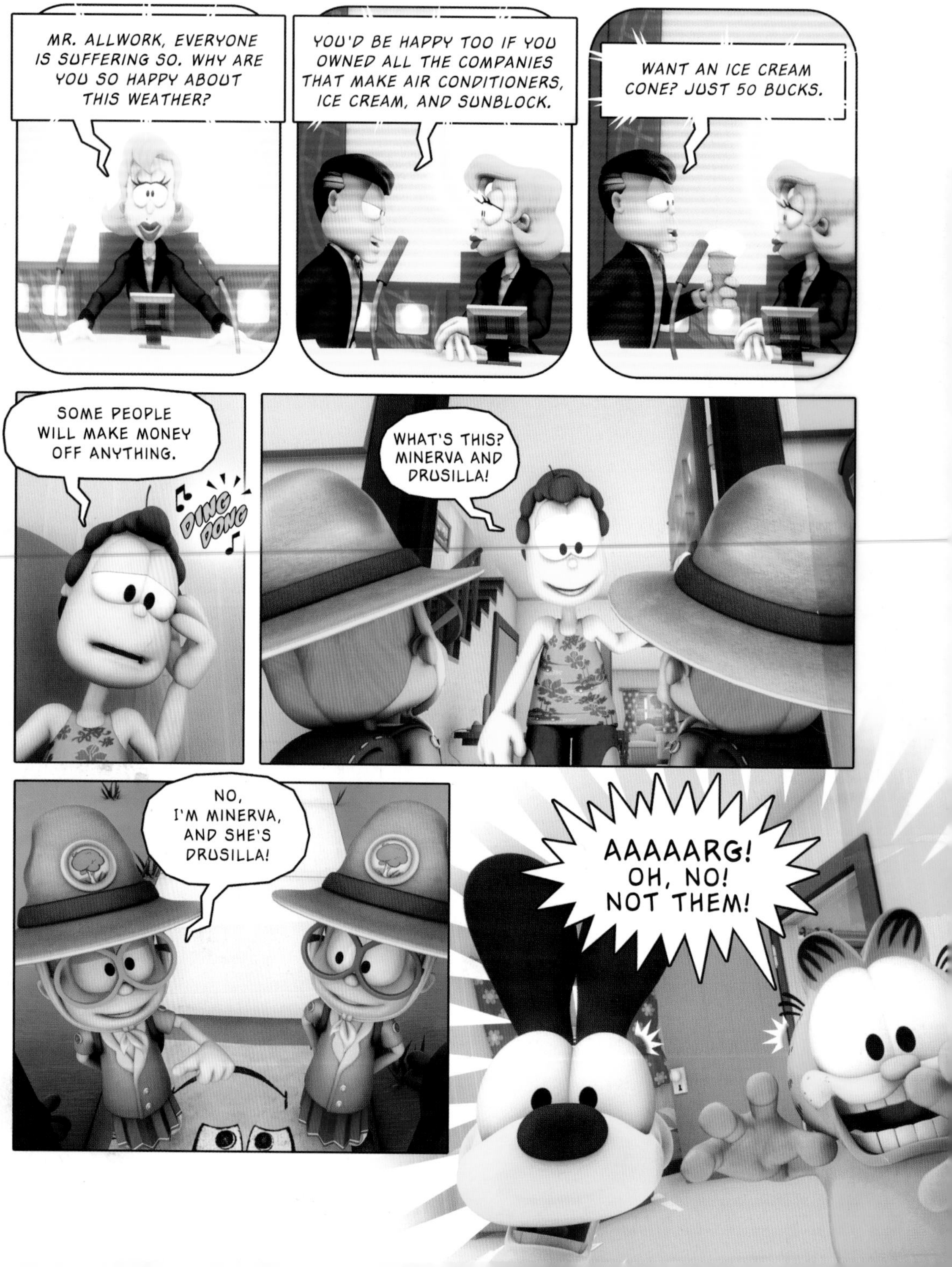
MR. ALLWORK, EVERYONE IS SUFFERING SO. WHY ARE YOU SO HAPPY ABOUT THIS WEATHER?
YOU'D BE HAPPY TOO IF YOU OWNED ALL THE COMPANIES THAT MAKE AIR CONDITIONERS, ICE CREAM, AND SUNBLOCK.
WANT AN ICE CREAM CONE? JUST 50 BUCKS.
SOME PEOPLE WILL MAKE MONEY OFF ANYTHING.
DING DONG
WHAT'S THIS? MINERVA AND DRUSILLA!
NO, I'M MINERVA, AND SHE'S DRUSILLA!
AAAAARG! OH, NO! NOT THEM!

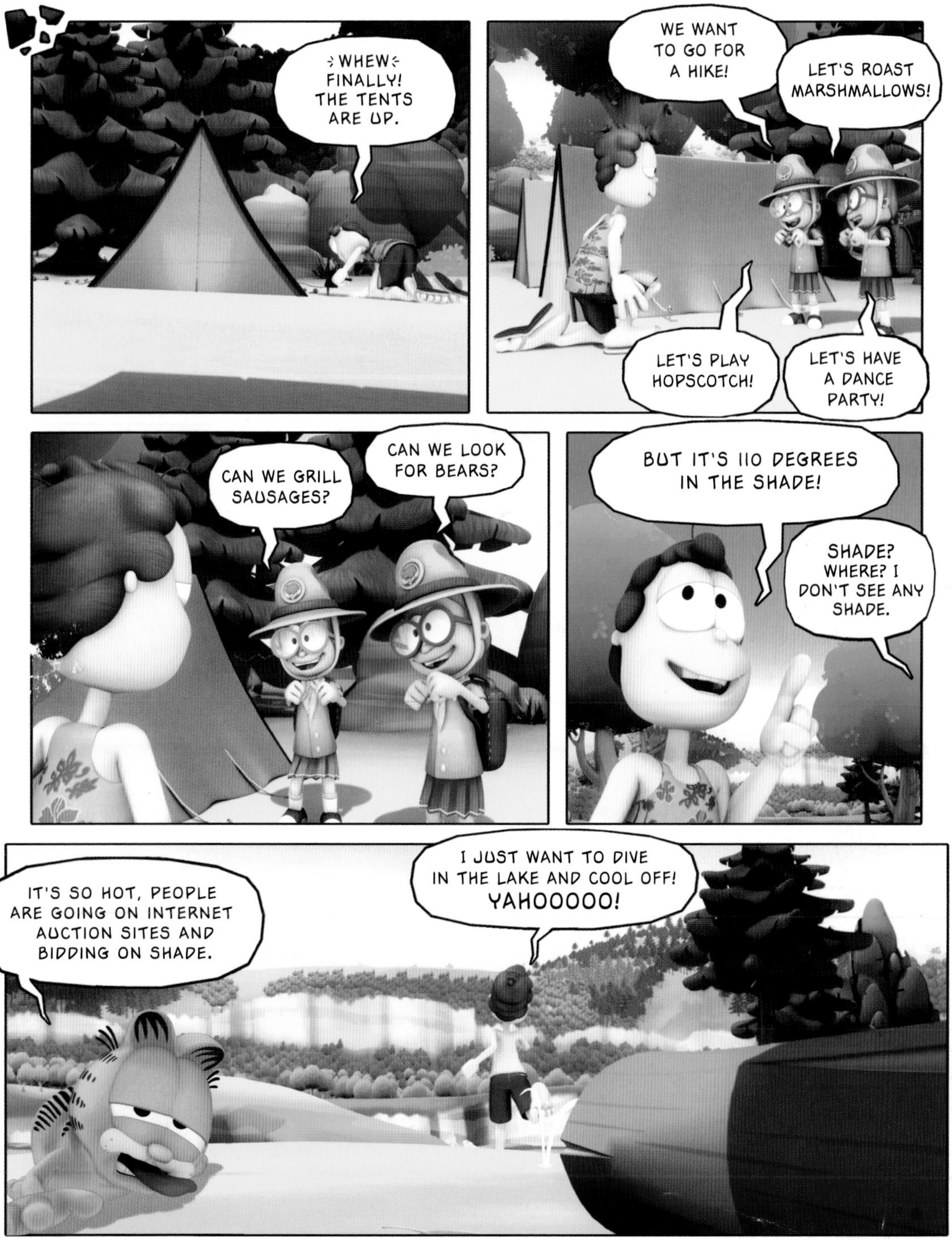
WHEW FINALLY! THE TENTS ARE UP.
WE WANT TO GO FOR A HIKE!
LET'S ROAST MARSHMALLOWS!
LET'S PLAY HOPSCOTCH!
LET'S HAVE A DANCE PARTY!
CAN WE GRILL SAUSAGES?
CAN WE LOOK FOR BEARS?
BUT IT'S 110 DEGREES IN THE SHADE!
SHADE? WHERE? I DON'T SEE ANY SHADE.
IT'S SO HOT, PEOPLE ARE GOING ON INTERNET AUCTION SITES AND BIDDING ON SHADE.
I JUST WANT TO DIVE IN THE LAKE AND COOL OFF! YAHOOOOO!

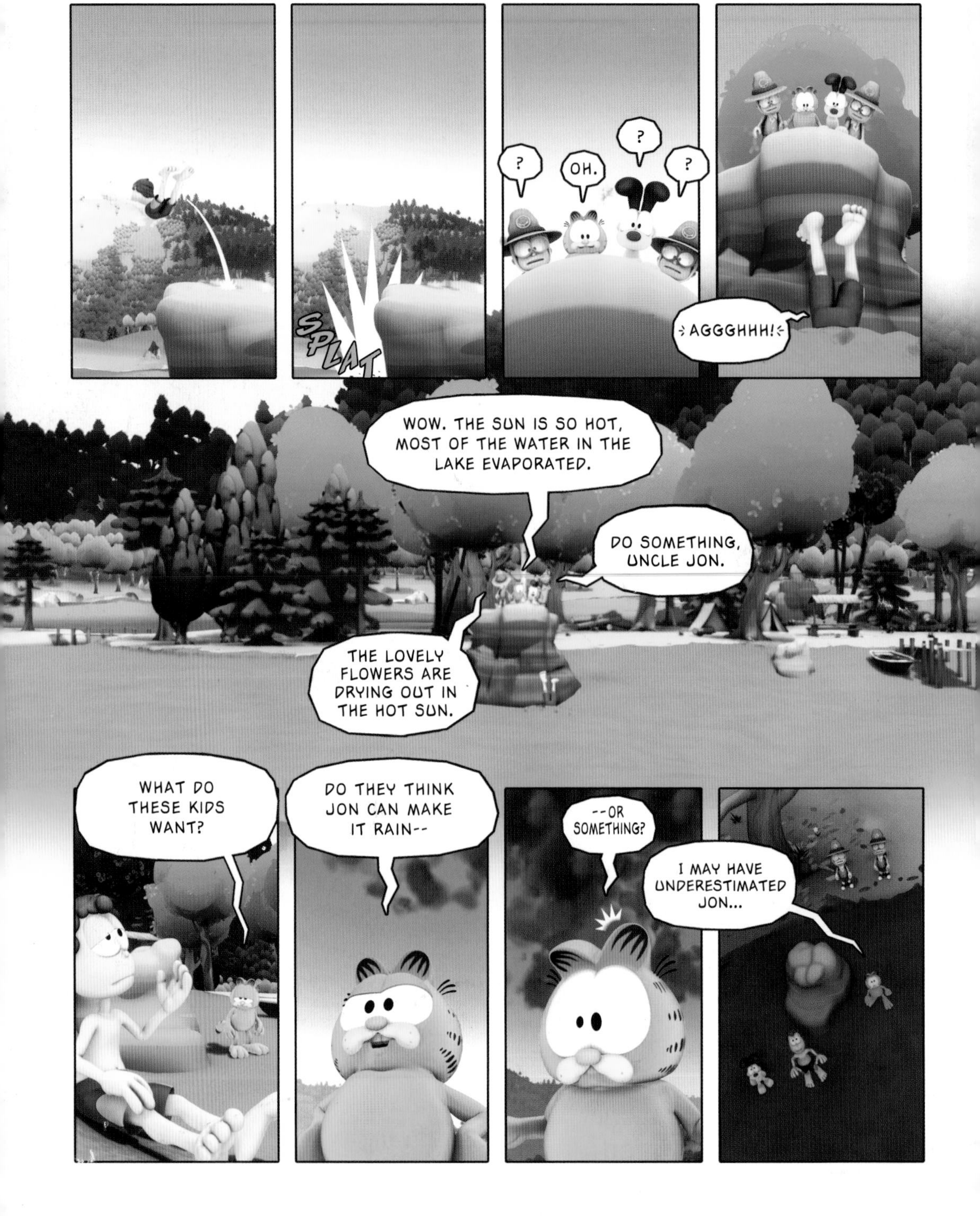
SPLAT
?
OH.
?
?
AGGGHHH!
WOW. THE SUN IS SO HOT, MOST OF THE WATER IN THE LAKE EVAPORATED.
DO SOMETHING, UNCLE JON.
THE LOVELY FLOWERS ARE DRYING OUT IN THE HOT SUN.
WHAT DO THESE KIDS WANT?
DO THEY THINK JON CAN MAKE IT RAIN--
--OR SOMETHING?
I MAY HAVE UNDERESTIMATED JON...

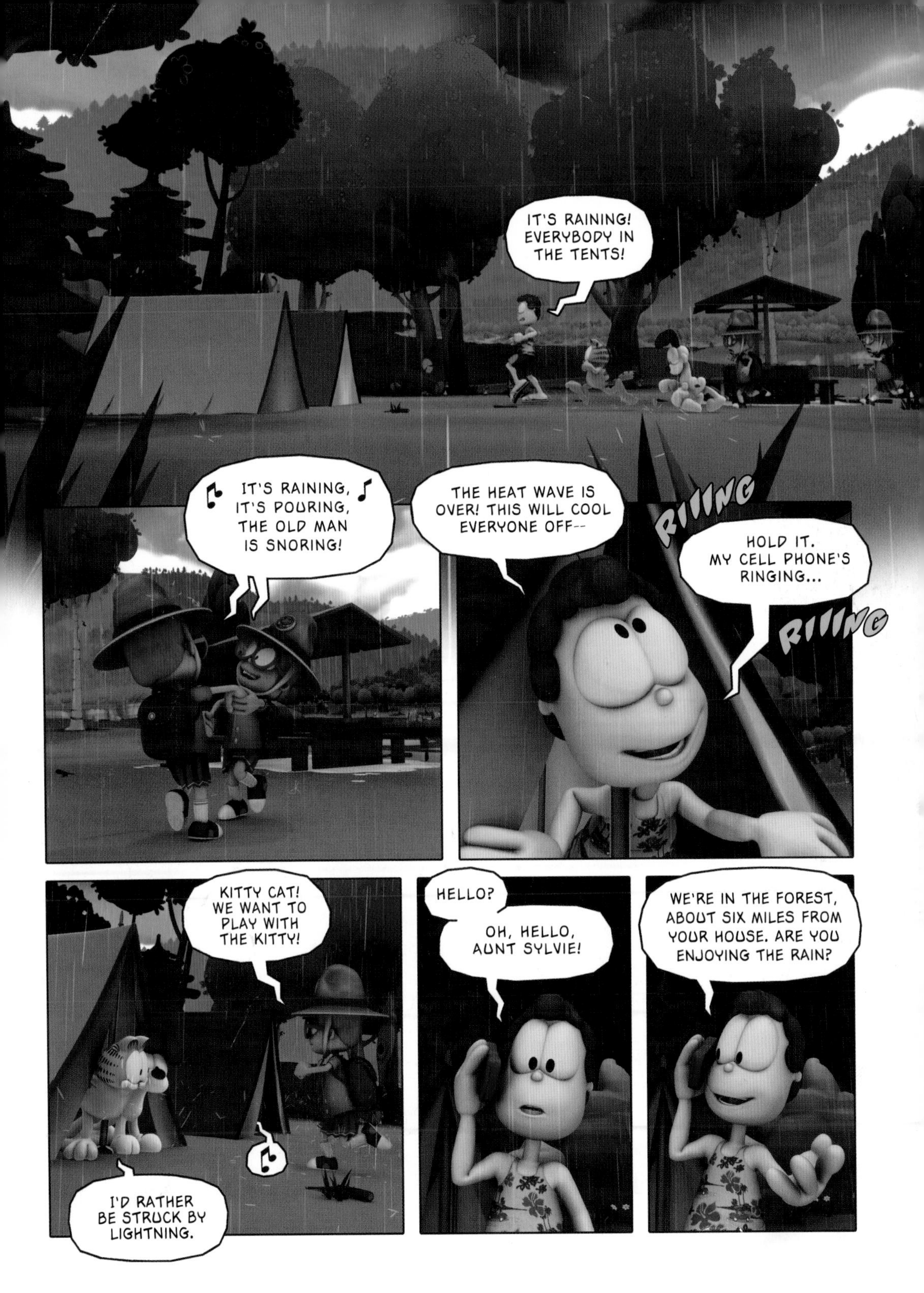
IT'S RAINING! EVERYBODY IN THE TENTS!
IT'S RAINING, IT'S POURING, THE OLD MAN IS SNORING!
THE HEAT WAVE IS OVER! THIS WILL COOL EVERYONE OFF--
RIIING
HOLD IT. MY CELL PHONE'S RINGING...
RIIING
KITTY CAT! WE WANT TO PLAY WITH THE KITTY!
I'D RATHER BE STRUCK BY LIGHTNING.
HELLO?
OH, HELLO, AUNT SYLVIE!
WE'RE IN THE FOREST, ABOUT SIX MILES FROM YOUR HOUSE. ARE YOU ENJOYING THE RAIN?

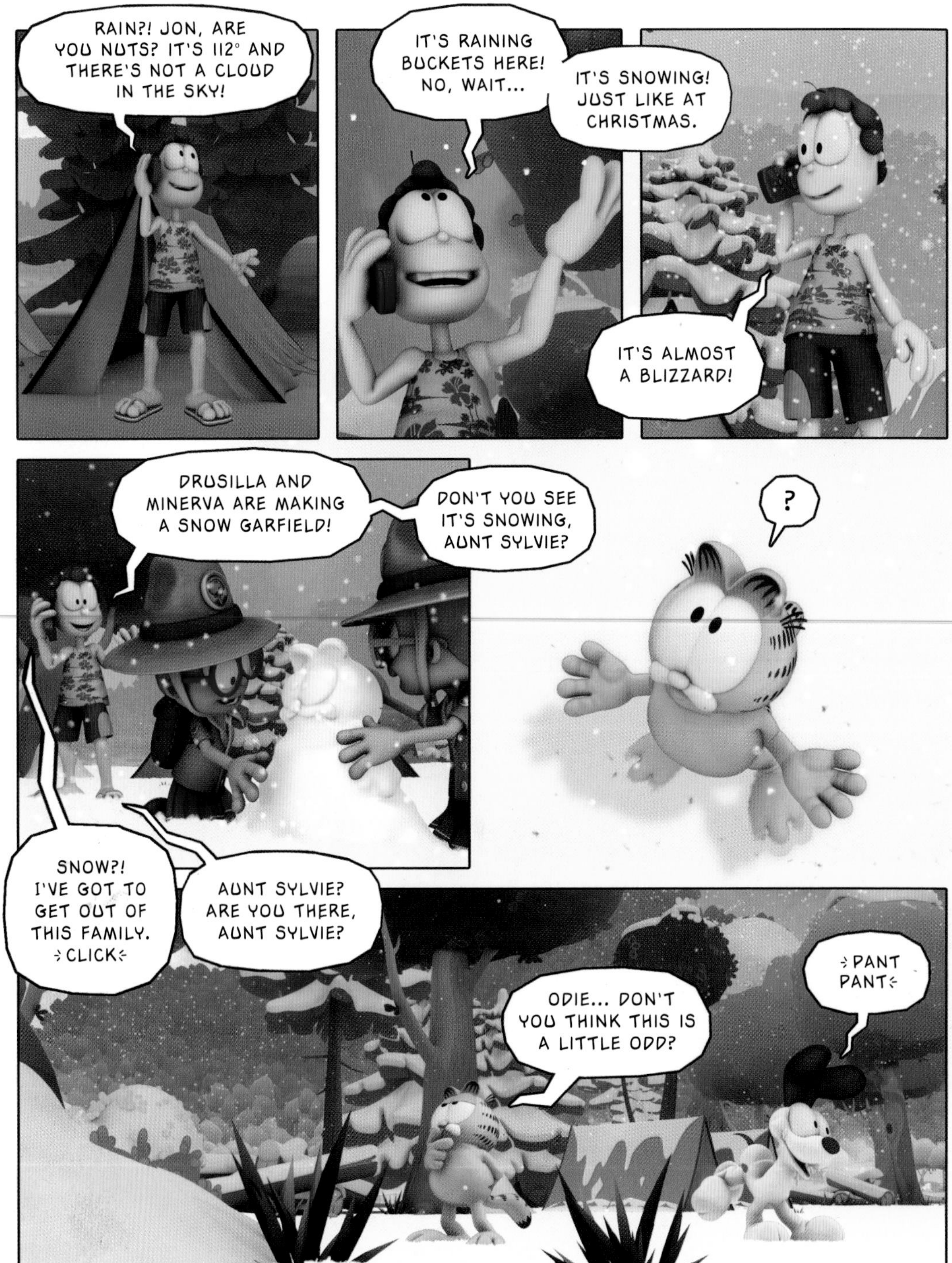
RAIN?! JON, ARE YOU NUTS? IT'S 112° AND THERE'S NOT A CLOUD IN THE SKY!
IT'S RAINING BUCKETS HERE! NO, WAIT...
IT'S SNOWING! JUST LIKE AT CHRISTMAS.
IT'S ALMOST A BLIZZARD!
DRUSILLA AND MINERVA ARE MAKING A SNOW GARFIELD!
DON'T YOU SEE IT'S SNOWING, AUNT SYLVIE?
?
SNOW?! I'VE GOT TO GET OUT OF THIS FAMILY. ⸗CLICK⸗
AUNT SYLVIE? ARE YOU THERE, AUNT SYLVIE?
ODIE... DON'T YOU THINK THIS IS A LITTLE ODD?
⸗PANT PANT⸗

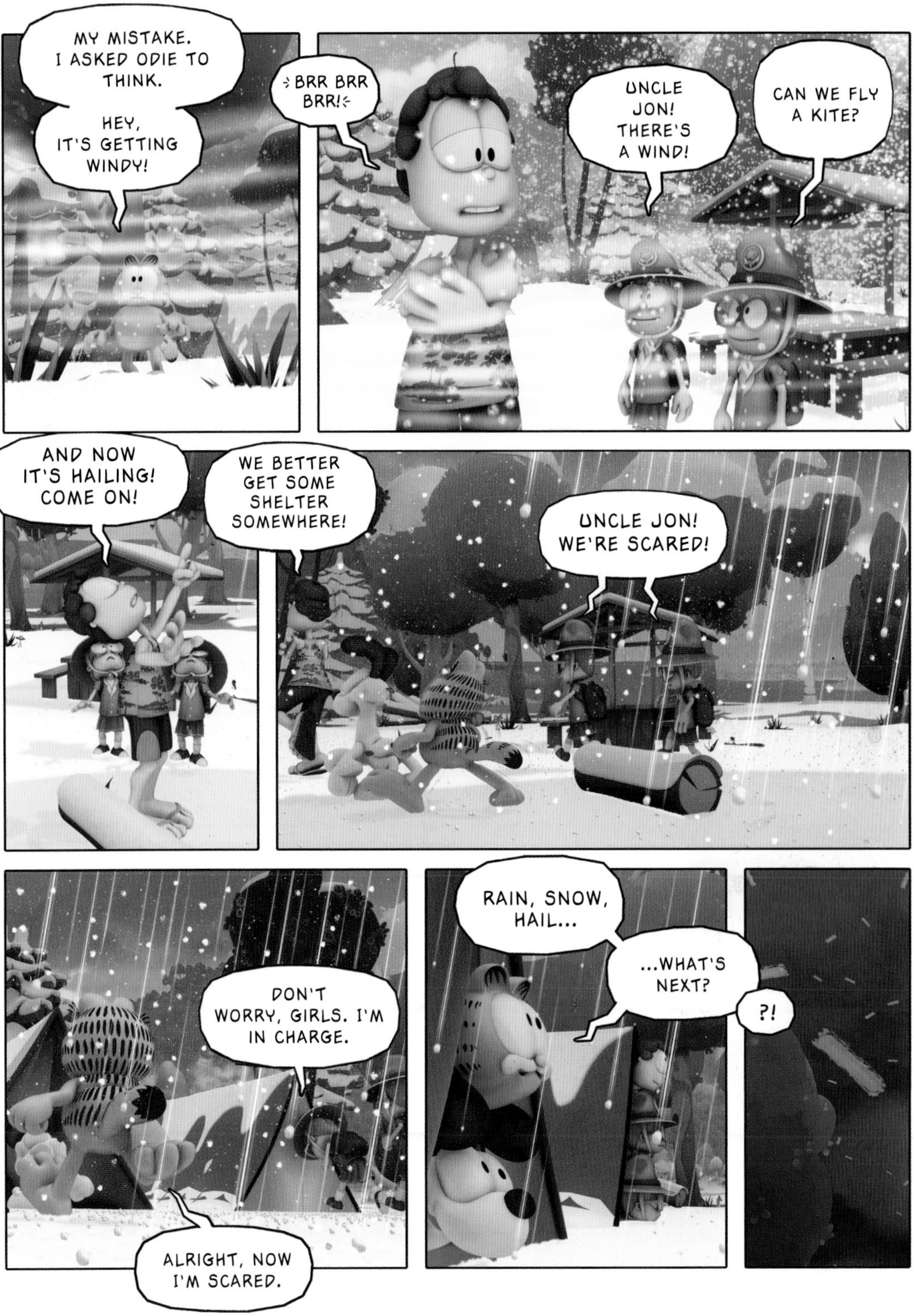
MY MISTAKE. I ASKED ODIE TO THINK.
HEY, IT'S GETTING WINDY!
BRR BRR BRR!
UNCLE JON! THERE'S A WIND!
CAN WE FLY A KITE?
AND NOW IT'S HAILING! COME ON!
WE BETTER GET SOME SHELTER SOMEWHERE!
UNCLE JON! WE'RE SCARED!
DON'T WORRY, GIRLS. I'M IN CHARGE.
ALRIGHT, NOW I'M SCARED.
RAIN, SNOW, HAIL...
...WHAT'S NEXT?
?!

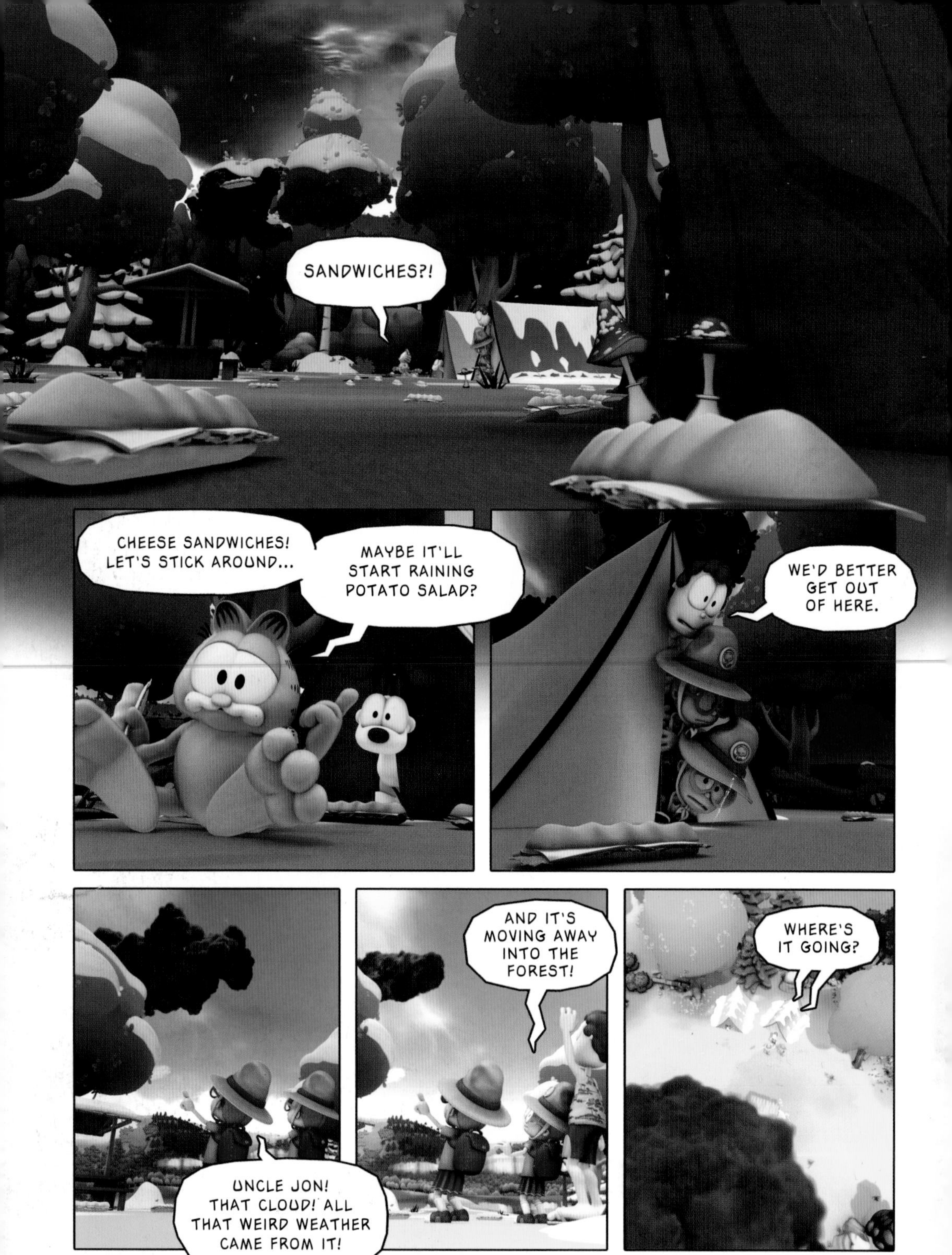
SANDWICHES?!
CHEESE SANDWICHES! LET'S STICK AROUND...
MAYBE IT'LL START RAINING POTATO SALAD?
WE'D BETTER GET OUT OF HERE.
UNCLE JON! THAT CLOUD! ALL THAT WEIRD WEATHER CAME FROM IT!
AND IT'S MOVING AWAY INTO THE FOREST!
WHERE'S IT GOING?

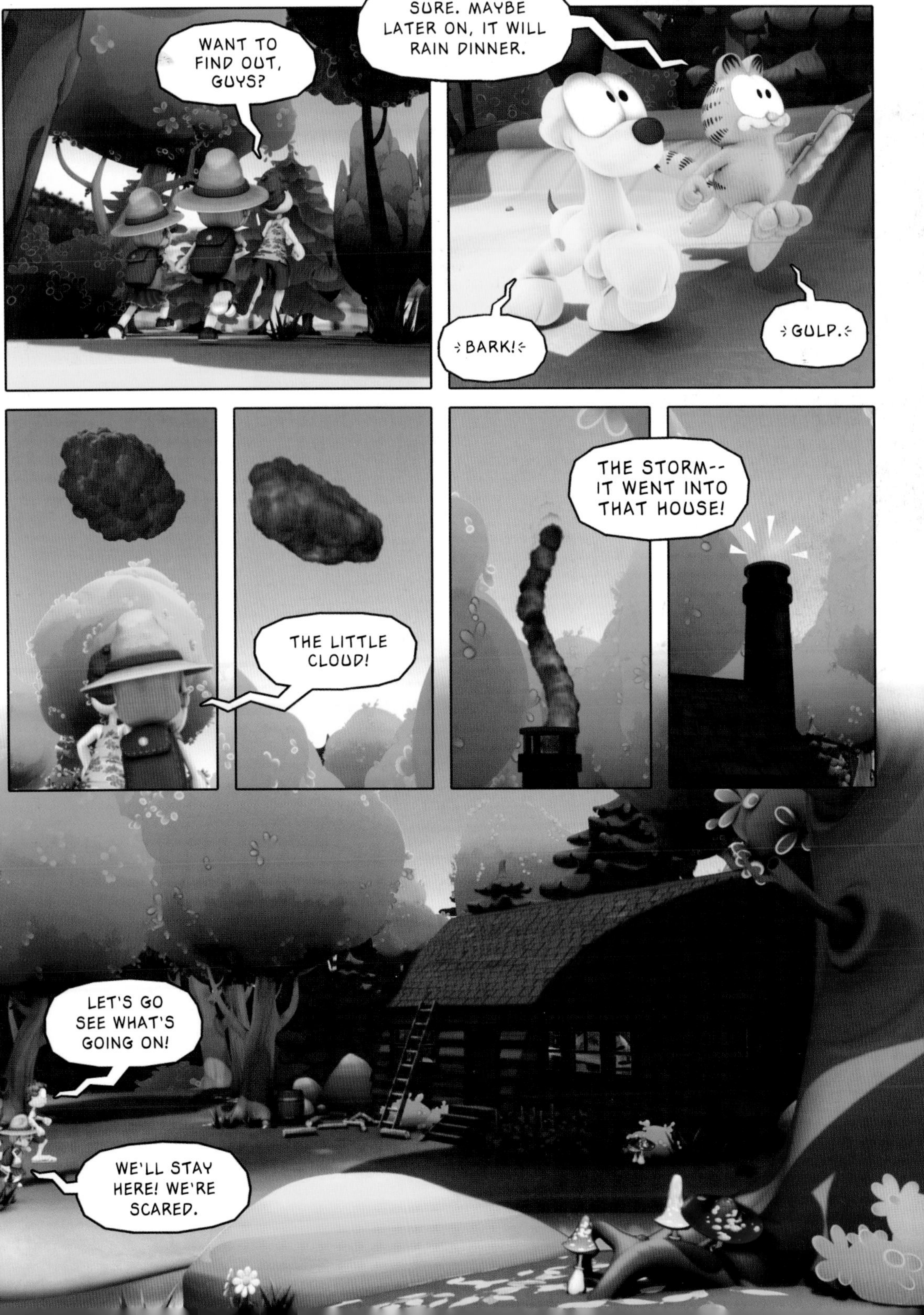
WANT TO FIND OUT, GUYS?
SURE. MAYBE LATER ON, IT WILL RAIN DINNER.
BARK!
GULP.
THE LITTLE CLOUD!
THE STORM-- IT WENT INTO THAT HOUSE!
LET'S GO SEE WHAT'S GOING ON!
WE'LL STAY HERE! WE'RE SCARED.

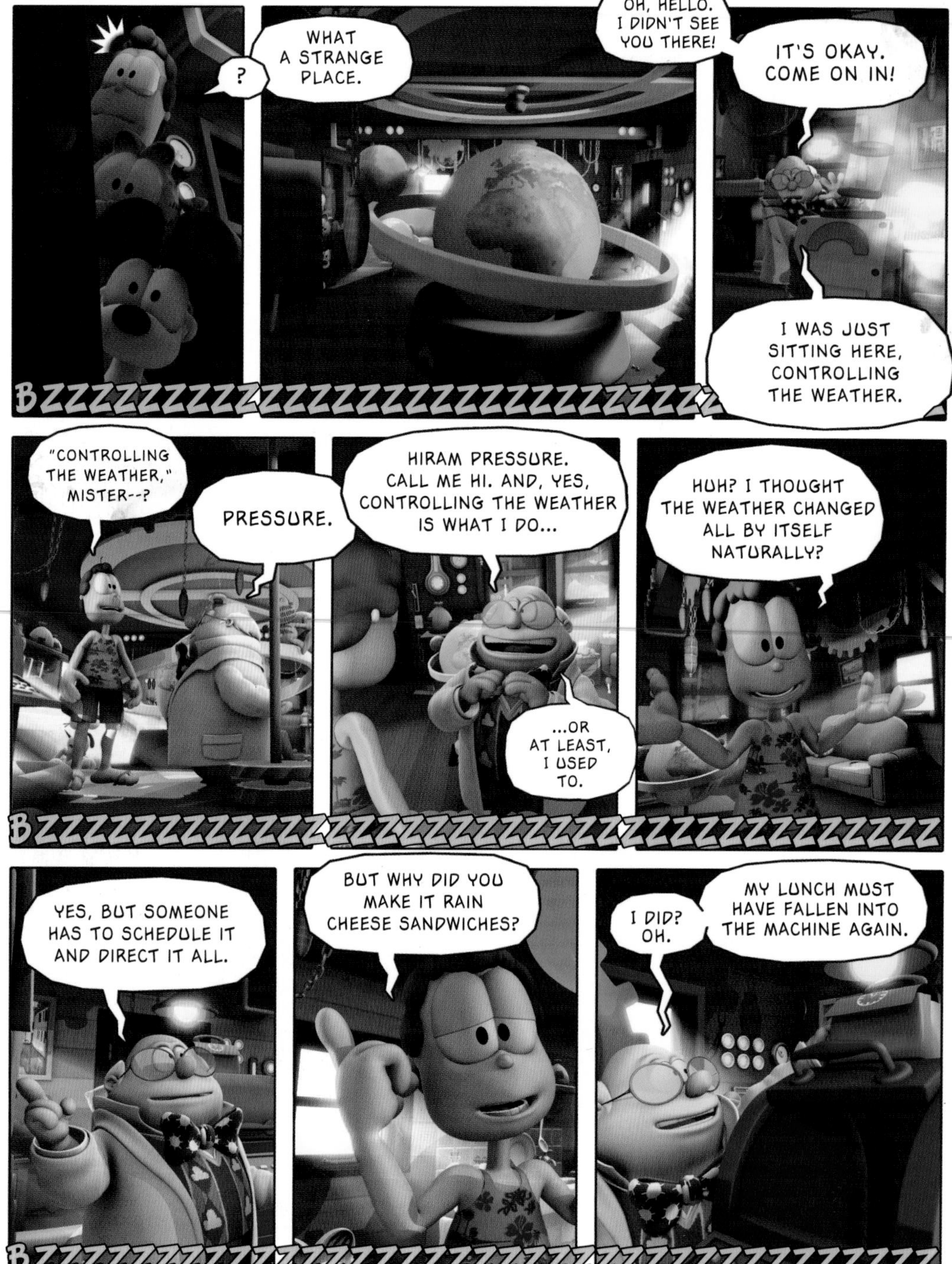
?
WHAT A STRANGE PLACE.
OH, HELLO. I DIDN'T SEE YOU THERE!
IT'S OKAY. COME ON IN!
I WAS JUST SITTING HERE, CONTROLLING THE WEATHER.
BZZZZZZZZZZZZZZZZZZZZZZZZZZZZZZZZZZ
"CONTROLLING THE WEATHER," MISTER--?
PRESSURE.
HIRAM PRESSURE. CALL ME HI. AND, YES, CONTROLLING THE WEATHER IS WHAT I DO...
...OR AT LEAST, I USED TO.
HUH? I THOUGHT THE WEATHER CHANGED ALL BY ITSELF NATURALLY?
BZZZZZZZZZZZZZZZZZZZZZZZZZZZZZZZZZZZZZZZZ
YES, BUT SOMEONE HAS TO SCHEDULE IT AND DIRECT IT ALL.
BUT WHY DID YOU MAKE IT RAIN CHEESE SANDWICHES?
I DID? OH.
MY LUNCH MUST HAVE FALLEN INTO THE MACHINE AGAIN.
BZZZZZZZZZZZZZZZZZZZZZZZZZZZZZZZZZZZZZZZZZ

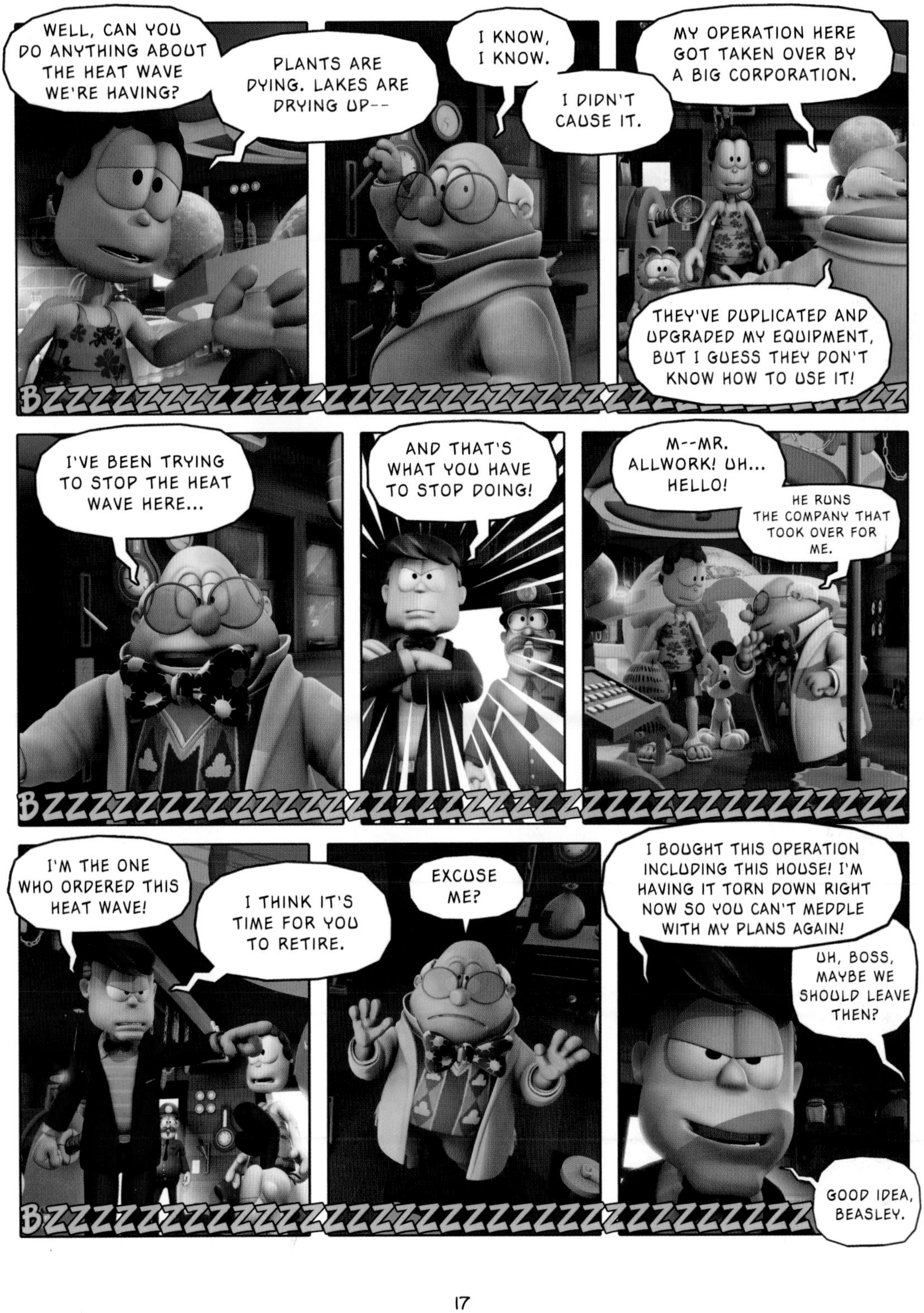
WELL, CAN YOU DO ANYTHING ABOUT THE HEAT WAVE WE'RE HAVING?
PLANTS ARE DYING. LAKES ARE DRYING UP--
I KNOW, I KNOW.
I DIDN'T CAUSE IT.
MY OPERATION HERE GOT TAKEN OVER BY A BIG CORPORATION.
THEY'VE DUPLICATED AND UPGRADED MY EQUIPMENT, BUT I GUESS THEY DON'T KNOW HOW TO USE IT!
BZZZZZZZZZZZZZZZZZZZZZZZZZZZZZZ
I'VE BEEN TRYING TO STOP THE HEAT WAVE HERE...
AND THAT'S WHAT YOU HAVE TO STOP DOING!
M--MR. ALLWORK! UH... HELLO!
HE RUNS THE COMPANY THAT TOOK OVER FOR ME.
BZZZZZZZZZZZZZZZZZZZZZZZZZZZZZZZZZZZZZZZZZZZ
I'M THE ONE WHO ORDERED THIS HEAT WAVE!
I THINK IT'S TIME FOR YOU TO RETIRE.
EXCUSE ME?
I BOUGHT THIS OPERATION INCLUDING THIS HOUSE! I'M HAVING IT TORN DOWN RIGHT NOW SO YOU CAN'T MEDDLE WITH MY PLANS AGAIN!
UH, BOSS, MAYBE WE SHOULD LEAVE THEN?
GOOD IDEA, BEASLEY.
BZZZZZZZZZZZZZZZZZZZZZZZZZZZZZZZZZZZZZZZZ

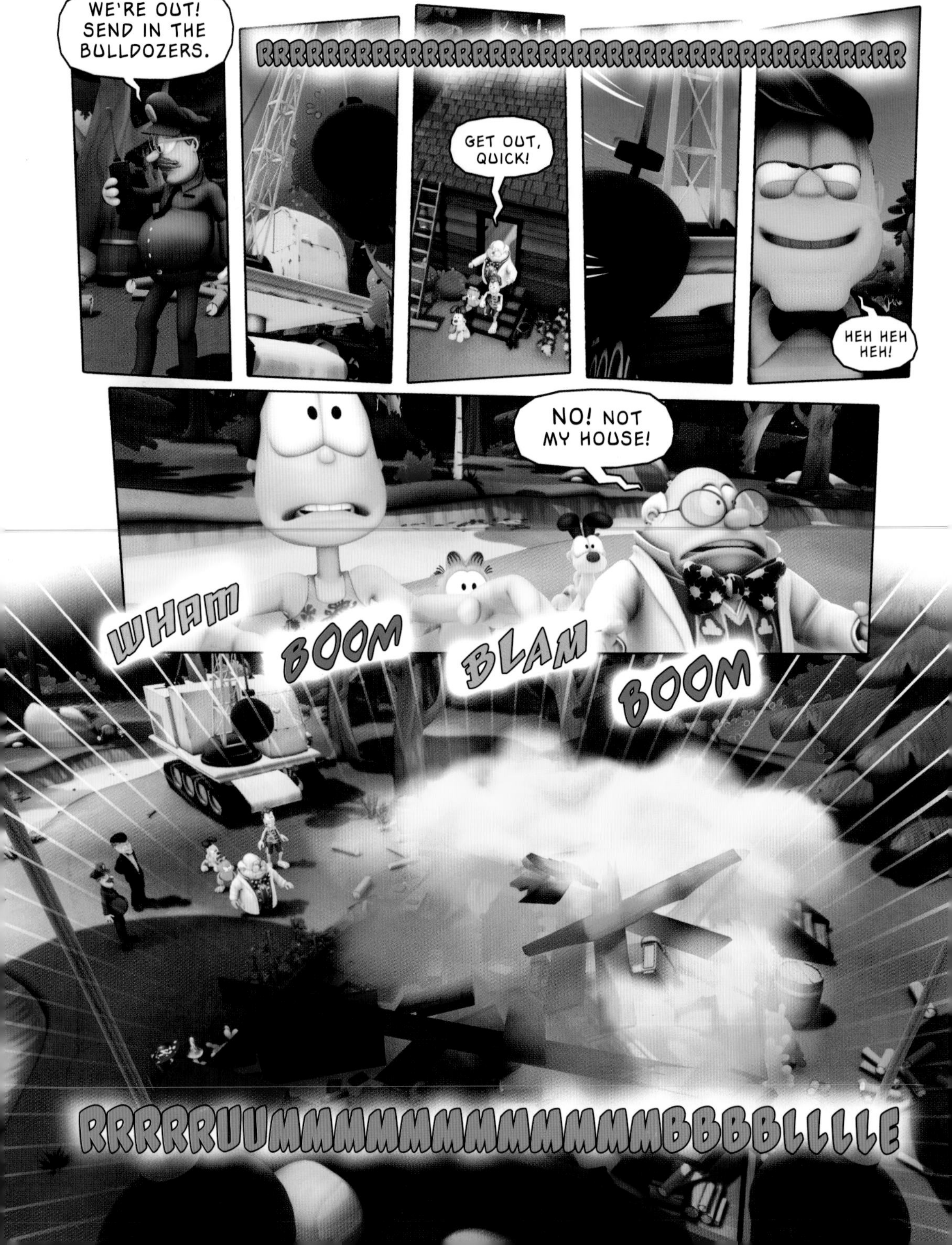
WE'RE OUT! SEND IN THE BULLDOZERS.
RRRRRRRRRRRRRRRRRRRRRRRRRRRRRRRRRRRRRRRRRRRR
GET OUT, QUICK!
HEH HEH HEH!
NO! NOT MY HOUSE!
WHAM
BOOM
BLAM
BOOM
RRRRRUUMMMMMMMMMMMMMMBBBBLLLLE

YOU DIDN'T HAVE TO DO THAT, YOU KNOW.

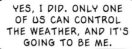

YES, I DID. ONLY ONE OF US CAN CONTROL THE WEATHER, AND IT'S GOING TO BE ME.

THERE ARE PEOPLE SUFFERING FROM THIS HOT WEATHER.

AND PEOPLE BUYING MY AIR CONDITIONERS AND MY SUN-BLOCK AND ALL THE OTHER THINGS I SELL.

THE HOTTER IT GETS, THE MORE I MAKE.

ICE CREAM CONE? FOR YOU, ONLY TWENTY-FIVE DOLLARS!

BEASLEY, GET THE CAR!

GRRRRRR

SEE YOU LATER. I HAVE TO GET BACK TO MY OFFICE AND RAISE THE PRICES ON EVERYTHING.

THIS IS ALL MY FAULT. I NEVER SHOULD HAVE LET HIM TAKE OVER.

UNCLE JON, WHERE'S GARFIELD?

YEAH! WHERE'S THE KITTY CAT?

OH, NO!

I SAW YOUR CAT AND DOG GET INTO MR. ALLWORK'S CAR JUST BEFORE IT LEFT.

456162342

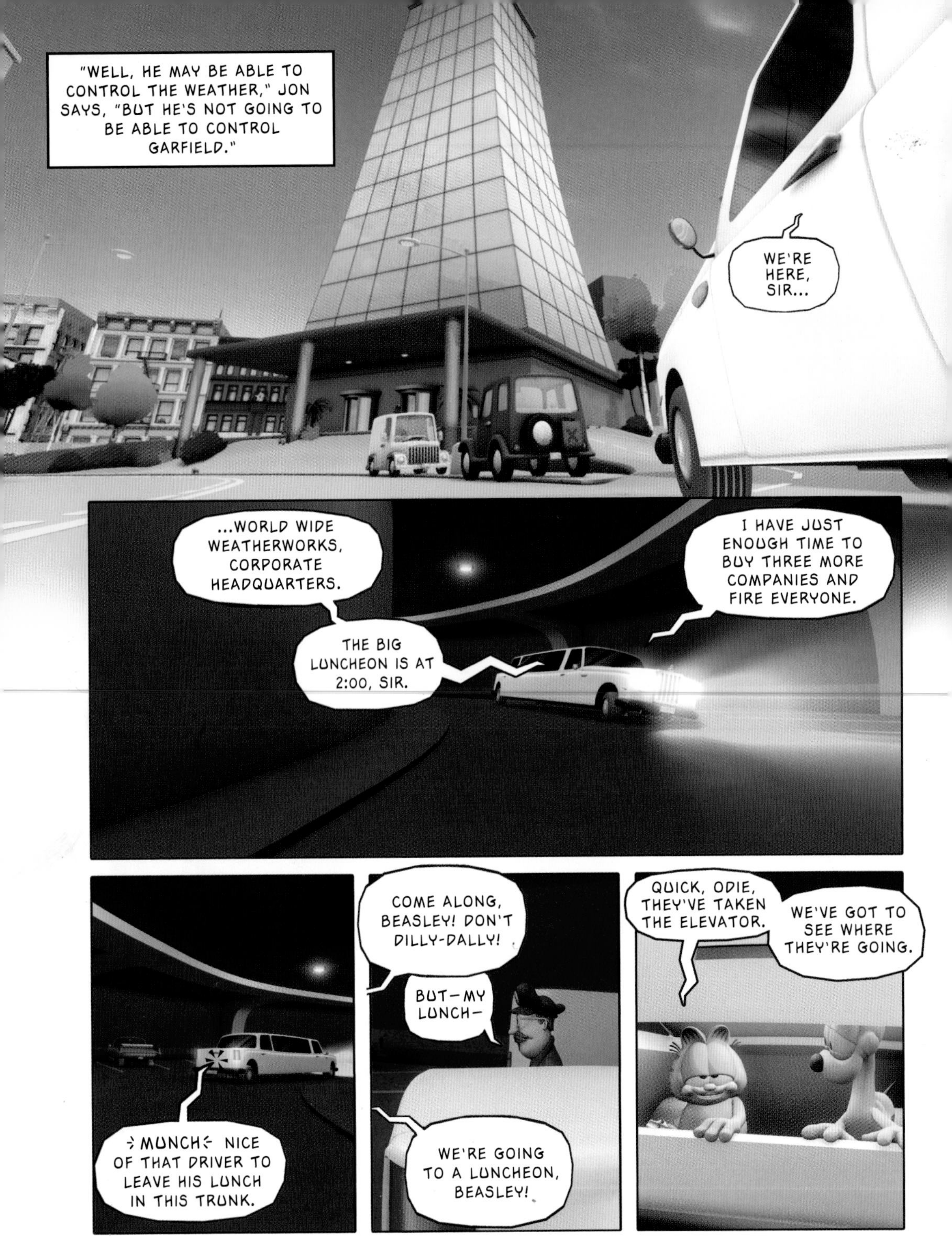
"WELL, HE MAY BE ABLE TO CONTROL THE WEATHER," JON SAYS, "BUT HE'S NOT GOING TO BE ABLE TO CONTROL GARFIELD."
WE'RE HERE, SIR...
...WORLD WIDE WEATHERWORKS, CORPORATE HEADQUARTERS.
THE BIG LUNCHEON IS AT 2:00, SIR.
I HAVE JUST ENOUGH TIME TO BUY THREE MORE COMPANIES AND FIRE EVERYONE.
⇉MUNCH⇇ NICE OF THAT DRIVER TO LEAVE HIS LUNCH IN THIS TRUNK.
COME ALONG, BEASLEY! DON'T DILLY-DALLY!
BUT—MY LUNCH—
WE'RE GOING TO A LUNCHEON, BEASLEY!
QUICK, ODIE, THEY'VE TAKEN THE ELEVATOR.
WE'VE GOT TO SEE WHERE THEY'RE GOING.

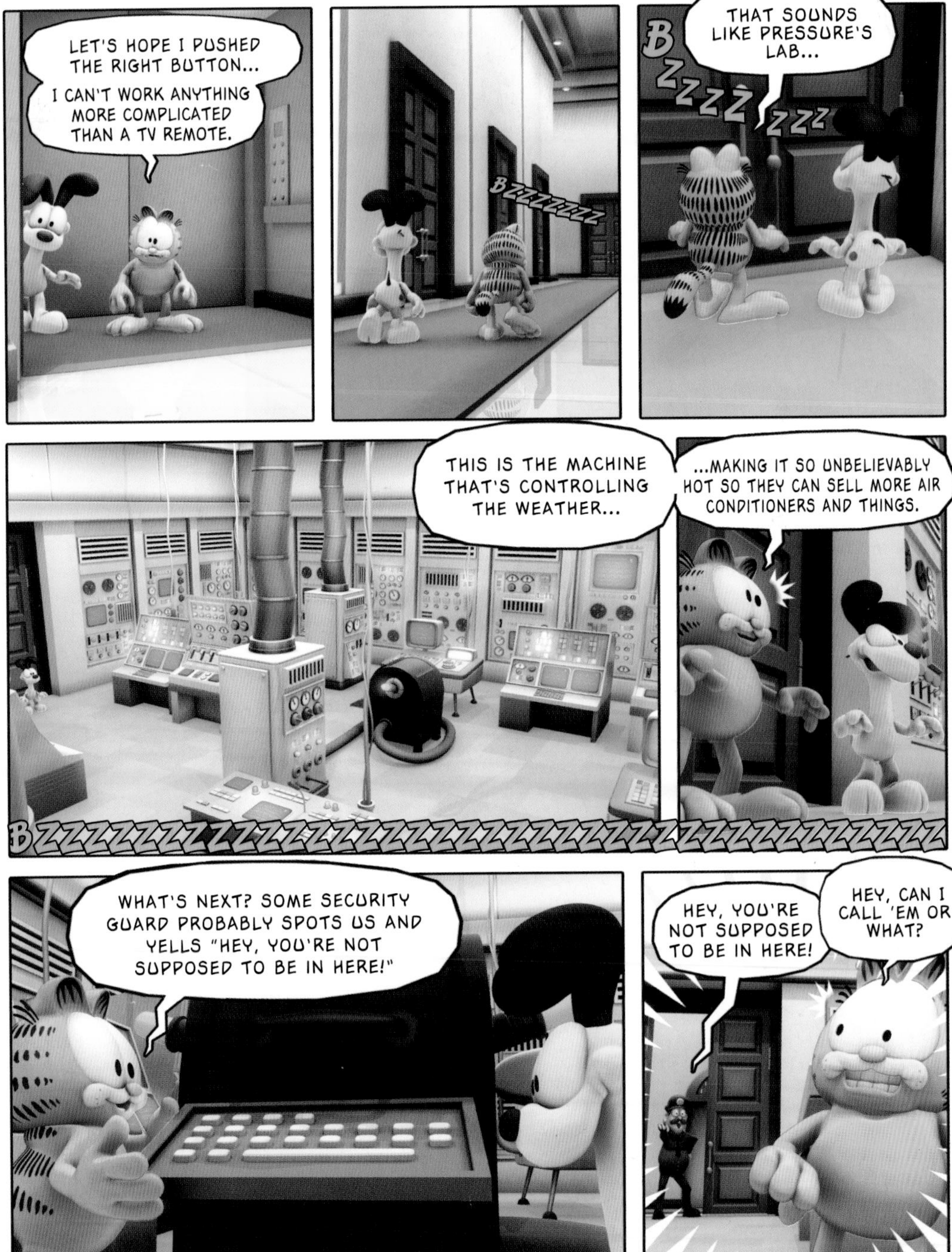

LET'S HOPE I PUSHED THE RIGHT BUTTON...
I CAN'T WORK ANYTHING MORE COMPLICATED THAN A TV REMOTE.
BZZZZZZZZ
BZZZZZZZ
THAT SOUNDS LIKE PRESSURE'S LAB...
THIS IS THE MACHINE THAT'S CONTROLLING THE WEATHER...
...MAKING IT SO UNBELIEVABLY HOT SO THEY CAN SELL MORE AIR CONDITIONERS AND THINGS.
BZZZZZZZZZZZZZZZZZZZZZZZZZZZZZZZZZZZZZZZZZZZZZZZZ
WHAT'S NEXT? SOME SECURITY GUARD PROBABLY SPOTS US AND YELLS "HEY, YOU'RE NOT SUPPOSED TO BE IN HERE!"
HEY, YOU'RE NOT SUPPOSED TO BE IN HERE!
HEY, CAN I CALL 'EM OR WHAT?

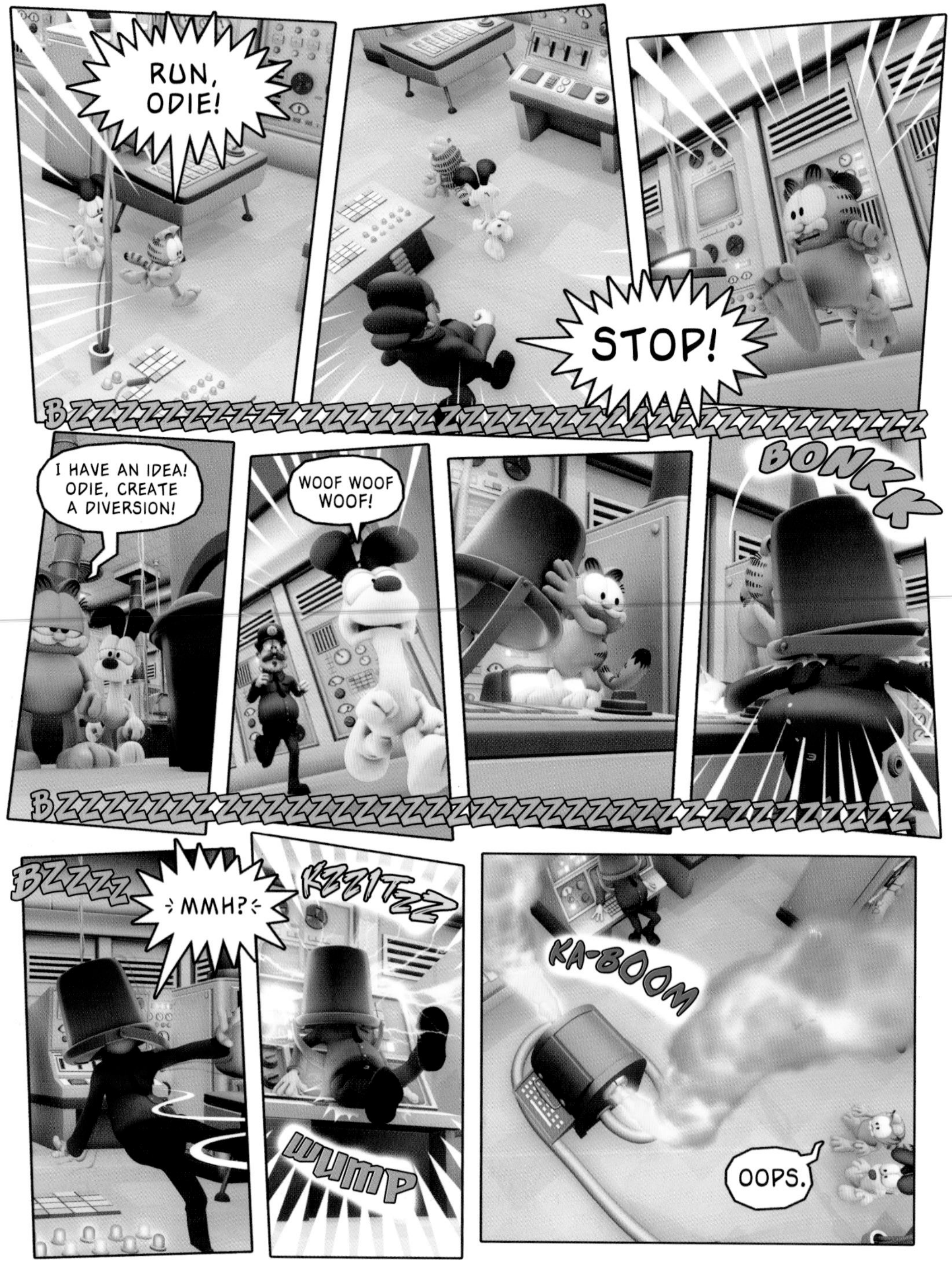
RUN, ODIE!
STOP!
BZZZZZZZZZZZZZZZZZZZZZZZZZZZZZZZZZZZZZZ
I HAVE AN IDEA! ODIE, CREATE A DIVERSION!
WOOF WOOF WOOF!
BONKK
BZZZZZZZZZZZZZZZZZZZZZZZZZZZZZZZZZZZZZZZ
BZZZZ
MMH?
KZZITZZ
WUMP
KA-BOOM
OOPS.

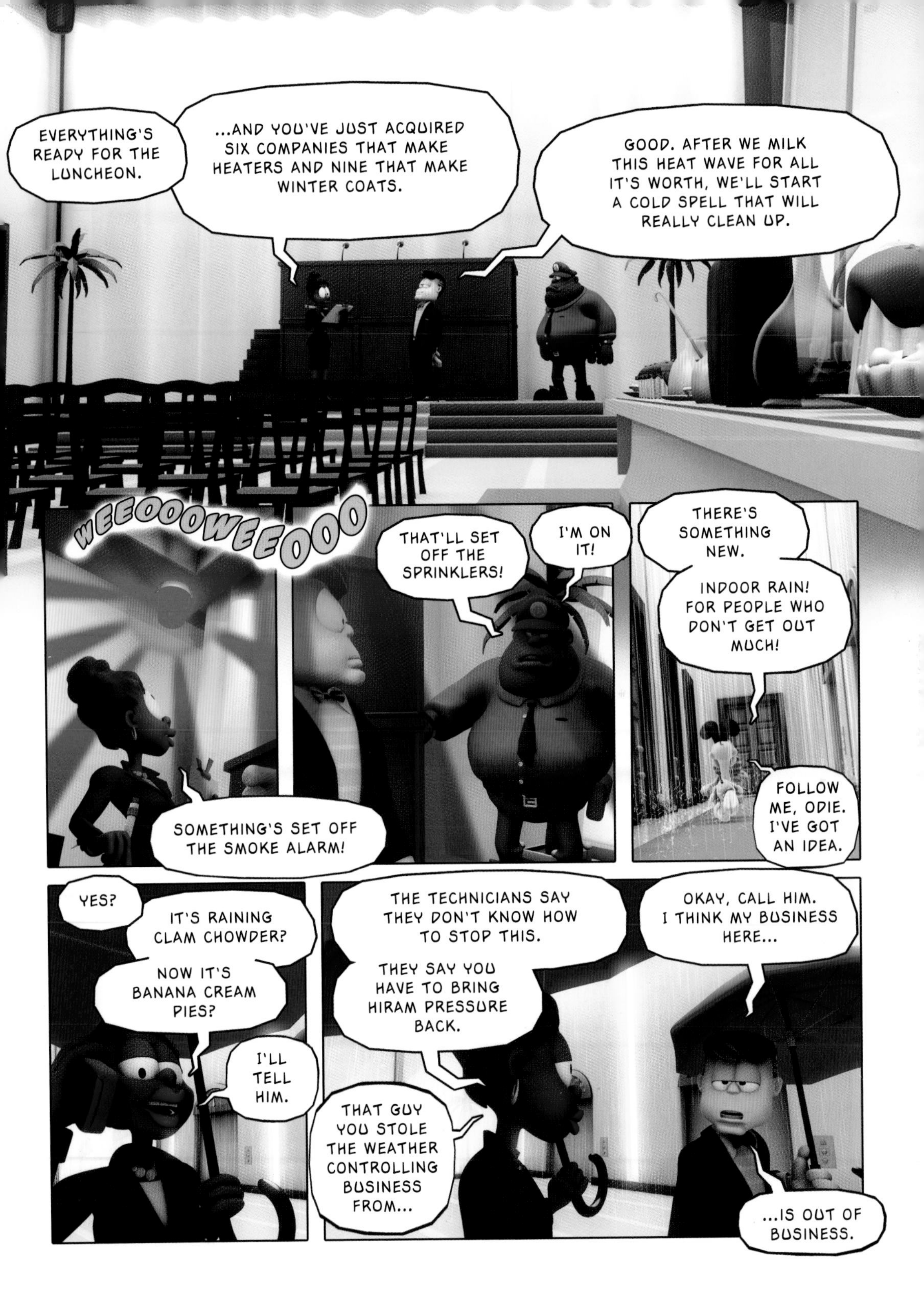
EVERYTHING'S READY FOR THE LUNCHEON.
...AND YOU'VE JUST ACQUIRED SIX COMPANIES THAT MAKE HEATERS AND NINE THAT MAKE WINTER COATS.
GOOD. AFTER WE MILK THIS HEAT WAVE FOR ALL IT'S WORTH, WE'LL START A COLD SPELL THAT WILL REALLY CLEAN UP.
WEEOOOWEEOOO
SOMETHING'S SET OFF THE SMOKE ALARM!
THAT'LL SET OFF THE SPRINKLERS!
I'M ON IT!
THERE'S SOMETHING NEW.
INDOOR RAIN! FOR PEOPLE WHO DON'T GET OUT MUCH!
FOLLOW ME, ODIE. I'VE GOT AN IDEA.
YES?
IT'S RAINING CLAM CHOWDER?
NOW IT'S BANANA CREAM PIES?
I'LL TELL HIM.
THE TECHNICIANS SAY THEY DON'T KNOW HOW TO STOP THIS.
THEY SAY YOU HAVE TO BRING HIRAM PRESSURE BACK.
THAT GUY YOU STOLE THE WEATHER CONTROLLING BUSINESS FROM...
OKAY, CALL HIM. I THINK MY BUSINESS HERE...
...IS OUT OF BUSINESS.

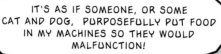
IT'S A MYSTERY, MR. ARBUCKLE...

IT'S AS IF SOMEONE, OR SOME CAT AND DOG, PURPOSEFULLY PUT FOOD IN MY MACHINES SO THEY WOULD MALFUNCTION!

MR. ALLWORK GAVE ME THE WHOLE OPERATION BACK.

I SHOULD HAVE THE HEAT WAVE ENDED WITHIN A DAY OR SO...

SO, YOU'LL BE CONTROLLING THE WEATHER AGAIN?

...I DON'T KNOW...

...I'VE BEEN THINKING...

...MAYBE I OUGHTA TRY LETTING NATURE TAKE ITS COURSE.

CONTROLLING THE WEATHER IS A LOT OF RESPONSIBILITY.

WELL, BEFORE YOU GIVE IT UP...

...MY CAT HAS ONE THING HE'D LIKE YOU TO DO...

SURE. ANYTHING FOR GARFIELD.

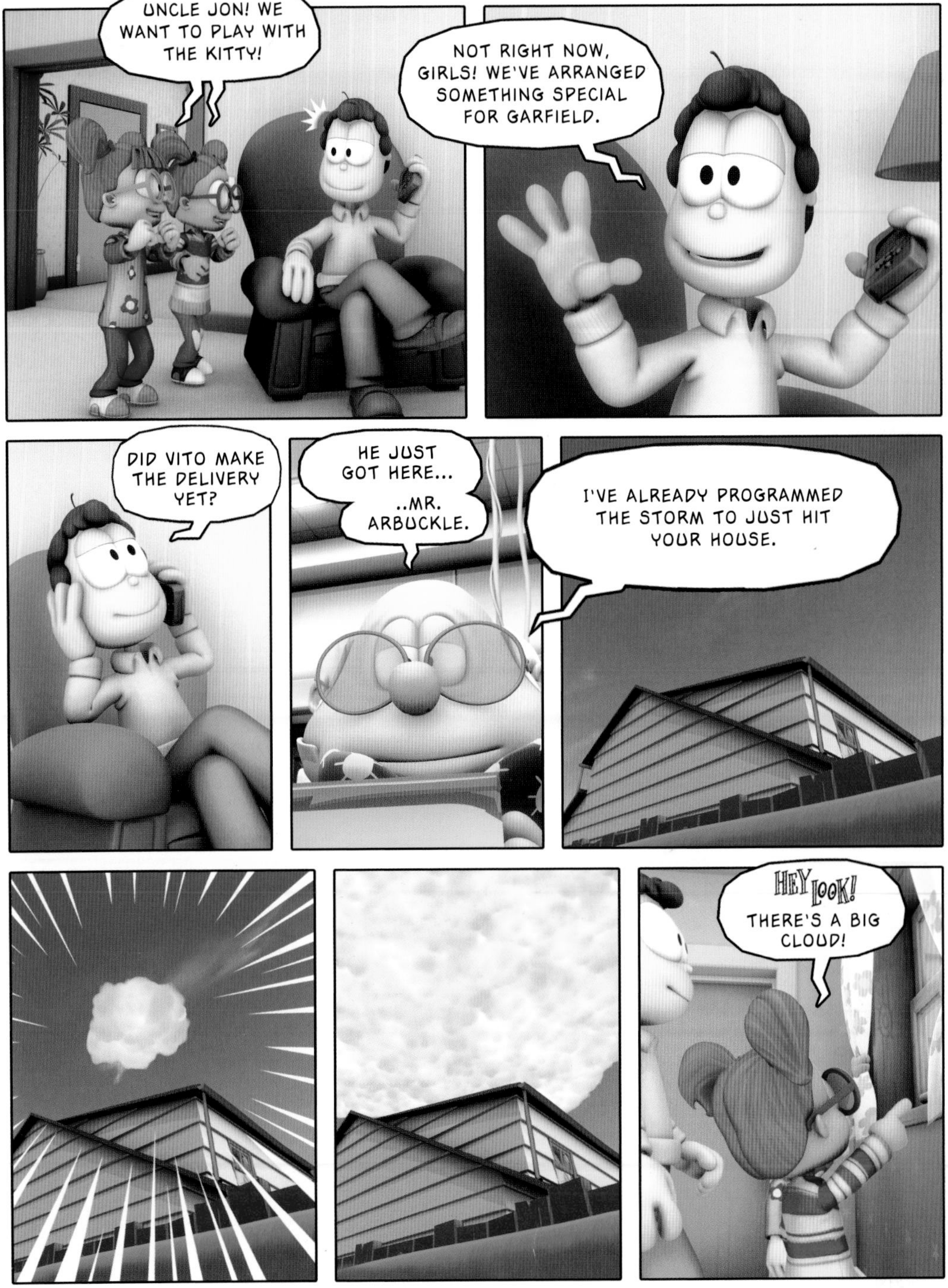

UNCLE JON! WE WANT TO PLAY WITH THE KITTY!
NOT RIGHT NOW, GIRLS! WE'VE ARRANGED SOMETHING SPECIAL FOR GARFIELD.
DID VITO MAKE THE DELIVERY YET?
HE JUST GOT HERE...
..MR. ARBUCKLE.
I'VE ALREADY PROGRAMMED THE STORM TO JUST HIT YOUR HOUSE.
HEY LOOK!
THERE'S A BIG CLOUD!

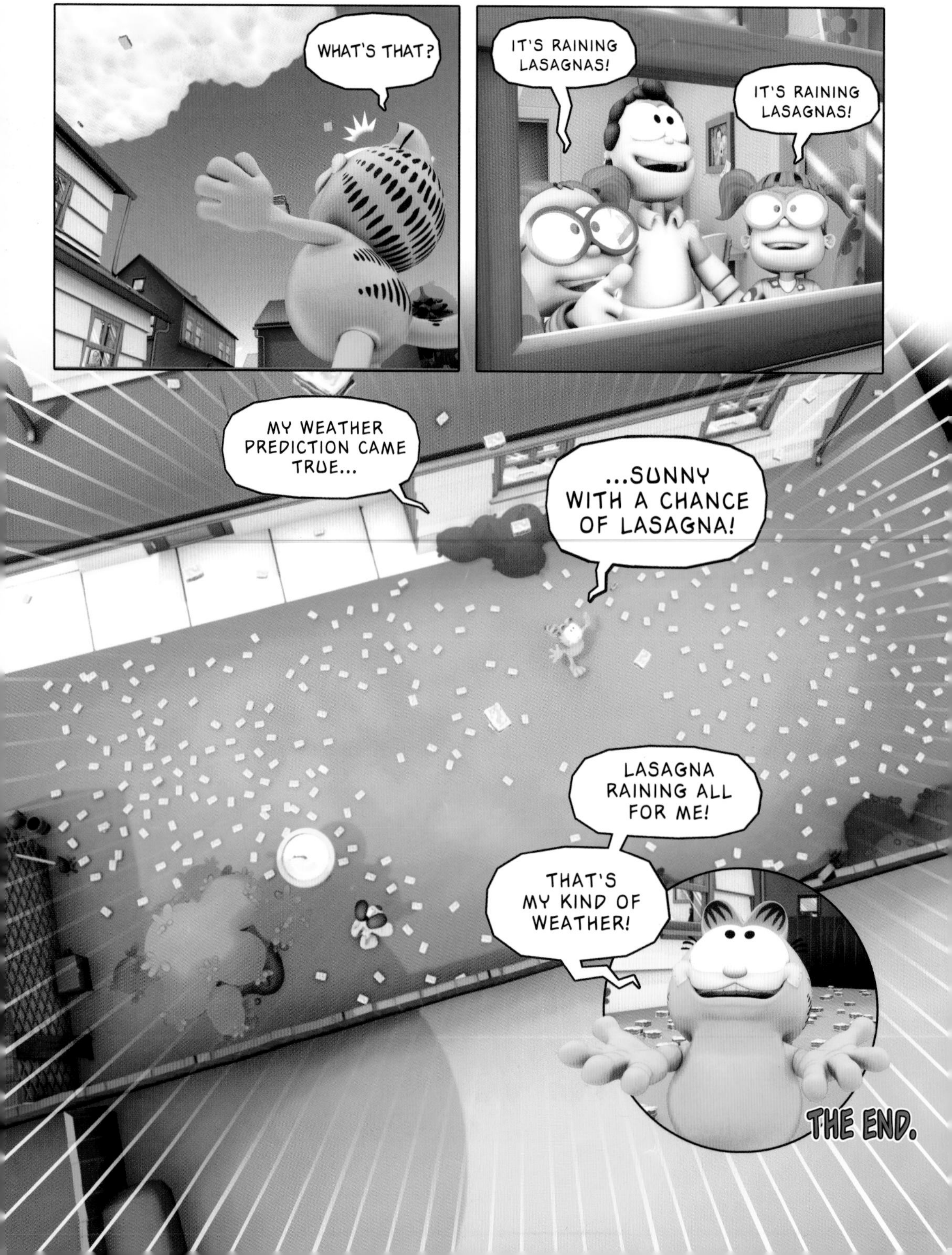
WHAT'S THAT?
IT'S RAINING LASAGNAS!
IT'S RAINING LASAGNAS!
MY WEATHER PREDICTION CAME TRUE...
...SUNNY WITH A CHANCE OF LASAGNA!
LASAGNA RAINING ALL FOR ME!
THAT'S MY KIND OF WEATHER!
THE END.

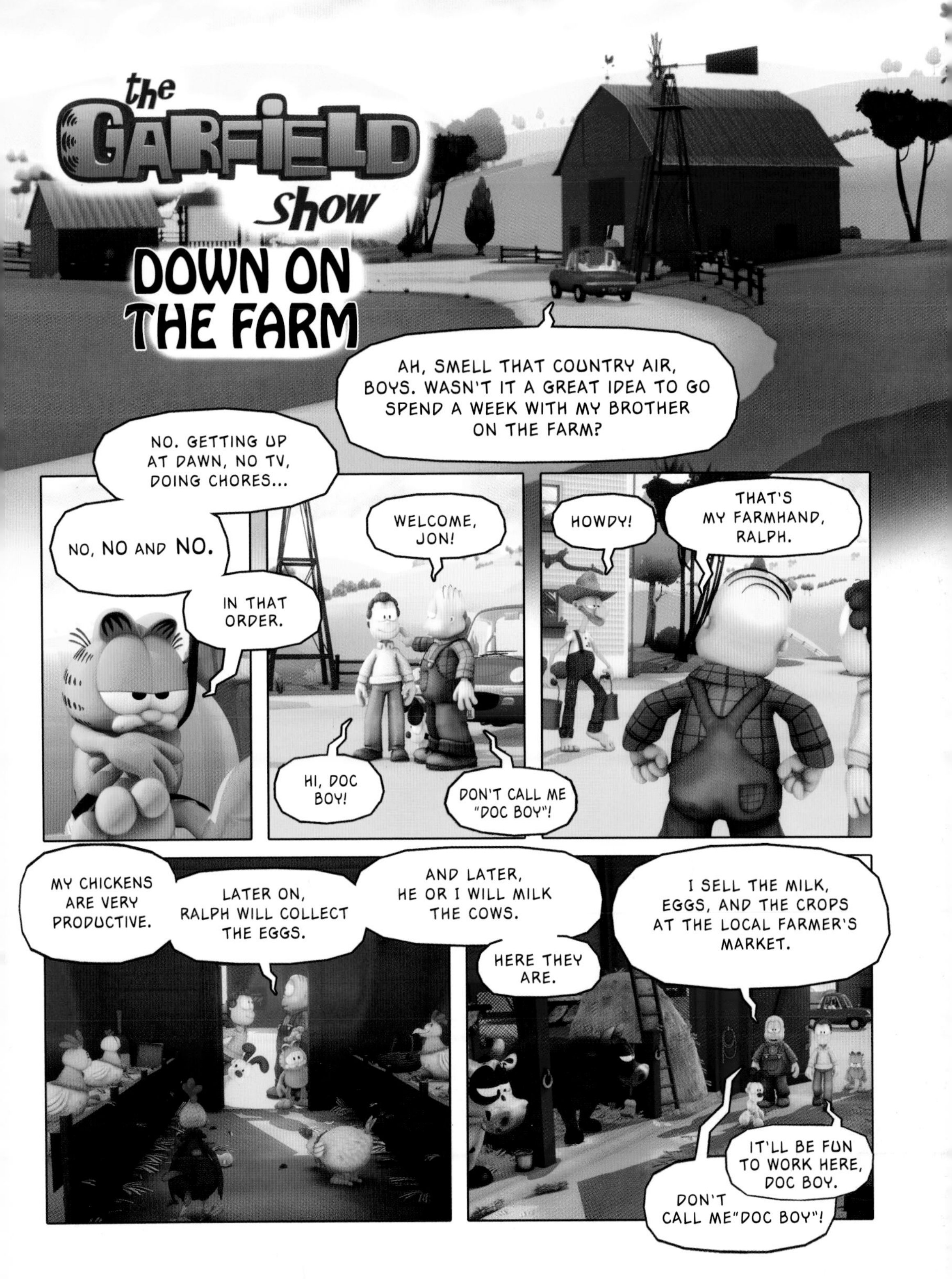

the GARFIELD show
DOWN ON THE FARM
AH, SMELL THAT COUNTRY AIR, BOYS. WASN'T IT A GREAT IDEA TO GO SPEND A WEEK WITH MY BROTHER ON THE FARM?
NO. GETTING UP AT DAWN, NO TV, DOING CHORES...
NO, NO AND NO.
IN THAT ORDER.
WELCOME, JON!
HI, DOC BOY!
DON'T CALL ME "DOC BOY"!
HOWDY!
THAT'S MY FARMHAND, RALPH.
MY CHICKENS ARE VERY PRODUCTIVE.
LATER ON, RALPH WILL COLLECT THE EGGS.
AND LATER, HE OR I WILL MILK THE COWS.
HERE THEY ARE.
I SELL THE MILK, EGGS, AND THE CROPS AT THE LOCAL FARMER'S MARKET.
IT'LL BE FUN TO WORK HERE, DOC BOY.
DON'T CALL ME"DOC BOY"!

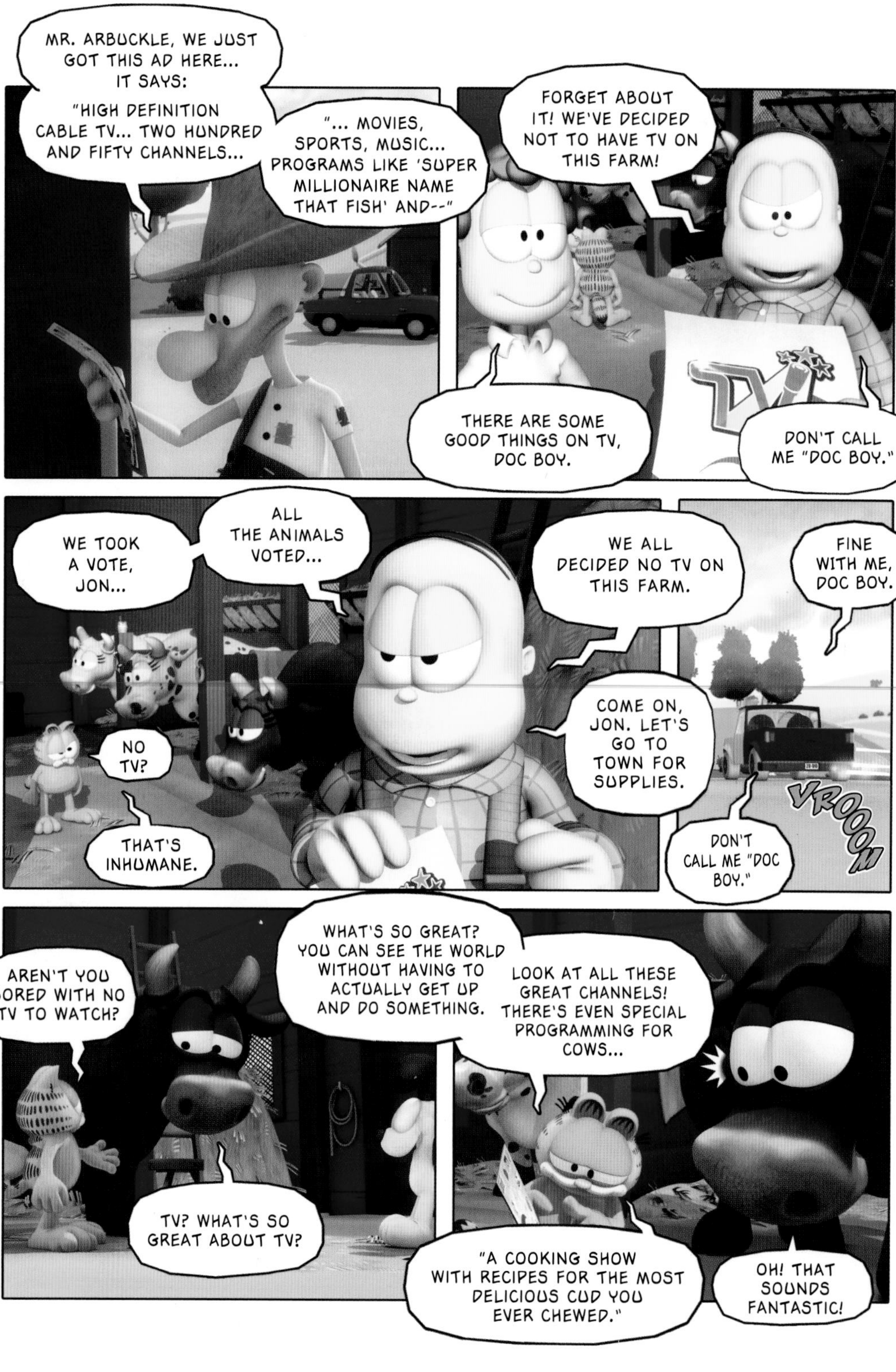
MR. ARBUCKLE, WE JUST GOT THIS AD HERE... IT SAYS:
"HIGH DEFINITION CABLE TV... TWO HUNDRED AND FIFTY CHANNELS...
"... MOVIES, SPORTS, MUSIC... PROGRAMS LIKE 'SUPER MILLIONAIRE NAME THAT FISH' AND--"
FORGET ABOUT IT! WE'VE DECIDED NOT TO HAVE TV ON THIS FARM!
THERE ARE SOME GOOD THINGS ON TV, DOC BOY.
DON'T CALL ME "DOC BOY."
WE TOOK A VOTE, JON...
ALL THE ANIMALS VOTED...
WE ALL DECIDED NO TV ON THIS FARM.
NO TV?
THAT'S INHUMANE.
COME ON, JON. LET'S GO TO TOWN FOR SUPPLIES.
FINE WITH ME, DOC BOY.
DON'T CALL ME "DOC BOY."
VROOOM
AREN'T YOU BORED WITH NO TV TO WATCH?
TV? WHAT'S SO GREAT ABOUT TV?
WHAT'S SO GREAT? YOU CAN SEE THE WORLD WITHOUT HAVING TO ACTUALLY GET UP AND DO SOMETHING.
LOOK AT ALL THESE GREAT CHANNELS! THERE'S EVEN SPECIAL PROGRAMMING FOR COWS...
"A COOKING SHOW WITH RECIPES FOR THE MOST DELICIOUS CUD YOU EVER CHEWED."
OH! THAT SOUNDS FANTASTIC!

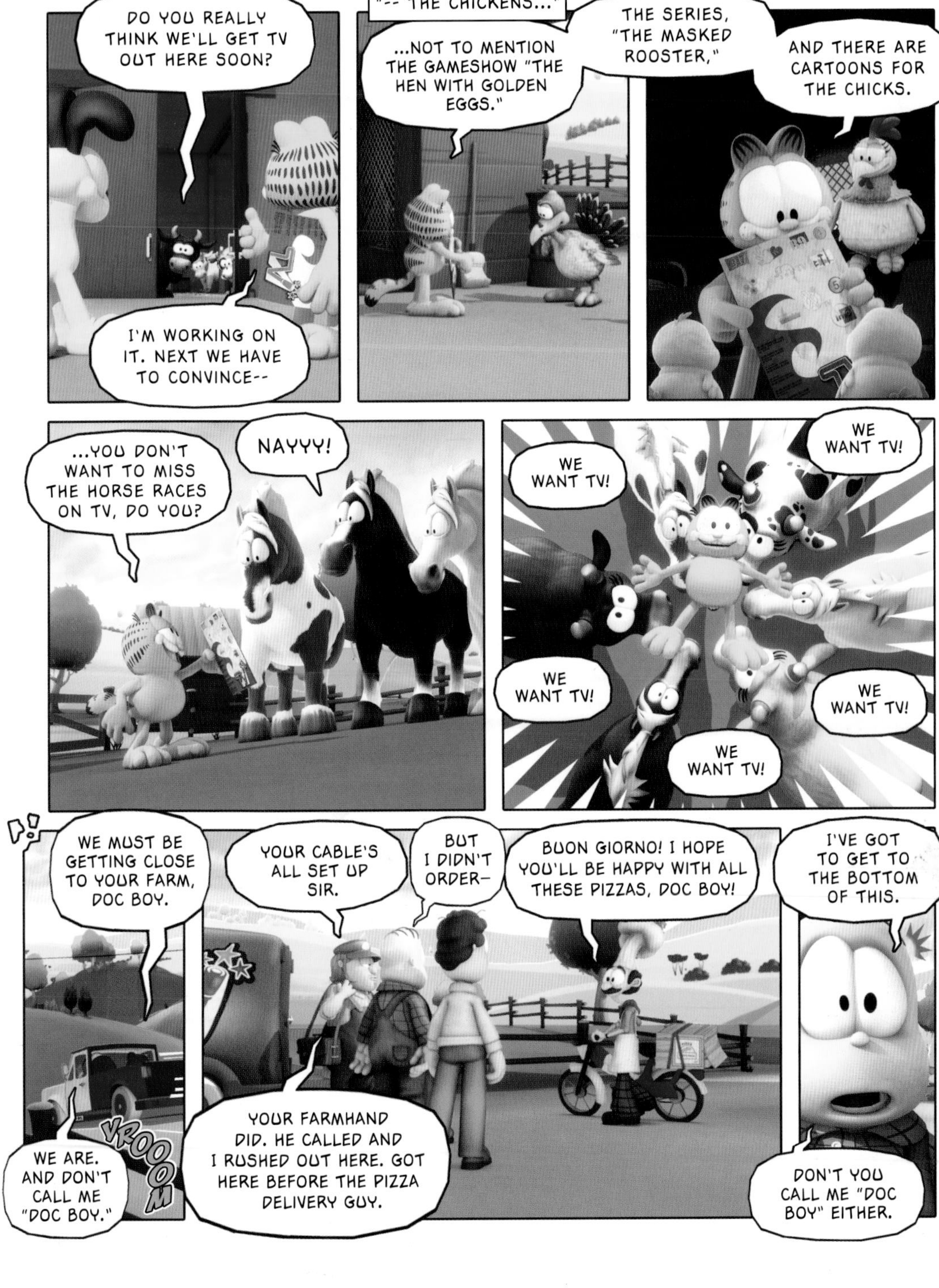

DO YOU REALLY THINK WE'LL GET TV OUT HERE SOON?
I'M WORKING ON IT. NEXT WE HAVE TO CONVINCE--
"-- THE CHICKENS..."
...NOT TO MENTION THE GAMESHOW "THE HEN WITH GOLDEN EGGS."
THE SERIES, "THE MASKED ROOSTER,"
AND THERE ARE CARTOONS FOR THE CHICKS.
...YOU DON'T WANT TO MISS THE HORSE RACES ON TV, DO YOU?
NAYYY!
WE WANT TV!
WE WANT TV!
WE WANT TV!
WE WANT TV!
WE WANT TV!
WE MUST BE GETTING CLOSE TO YOUR FARM, DOC BOY.
WE ARE. AND DON'T CALL ME "DOC BOY."
VROOOM
YOUR CABLE'S ALL SET UP SIR.
BUT I DIDN'T ORDER–
YOUR FARMHAND DID. HE CALLED AND I RUSHED OUT HERE. GOT HERE BEFORE THE PIZZA DELIVERY GUY.
BUON GIORNO! I HOPE YOU'LL BE HAPPY WITH ALL THESE PIZZAS, DOC BOY!
I'VE GOT TO GET TO THE BOTTOM OF THIS.
DON'T YOU CALL ME "DOC BOY" EITHER.

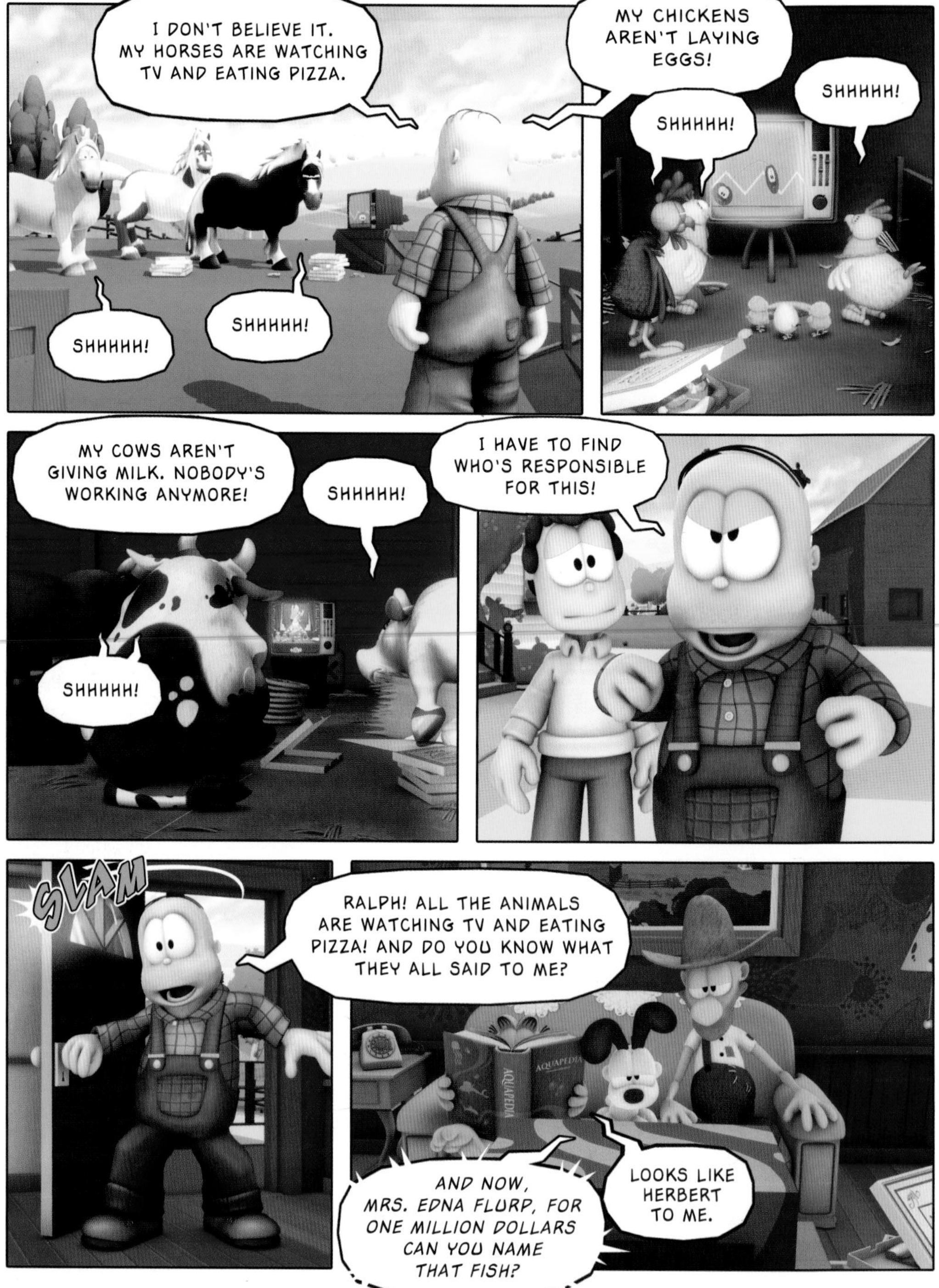
I DON'T BELIEVE IT. MY HORSES ARE WATCHING TV AND EATING PIZZA.
SHHHHH!
SHHHHH!
MY CHICKENS AREN'T LAYING EGGS!
SHHHHH!
SHHHHH!
MY COWS AREN'T GIVING MILK. NOBODY'S WORKING ANYMORE!
SHHHHH!
SHHHHH!
I HAVE TO FIND WHO'S RESPONSIBLE FOR THIS!
SLAM
RALPH! ALL THE ANIMALS ARE WATCHING TV AND EATING PIZZA! AND DO YOU KNOW WHAT THEY ALL SAID TO ME?
AQUAPEDIA
AND NOW, MRS. EDNA FLURP, FOR ONE MILLION DOLLARS CAN YOU NAME THAT FISH?
LOOKS LIKE HERBERT TO ME.

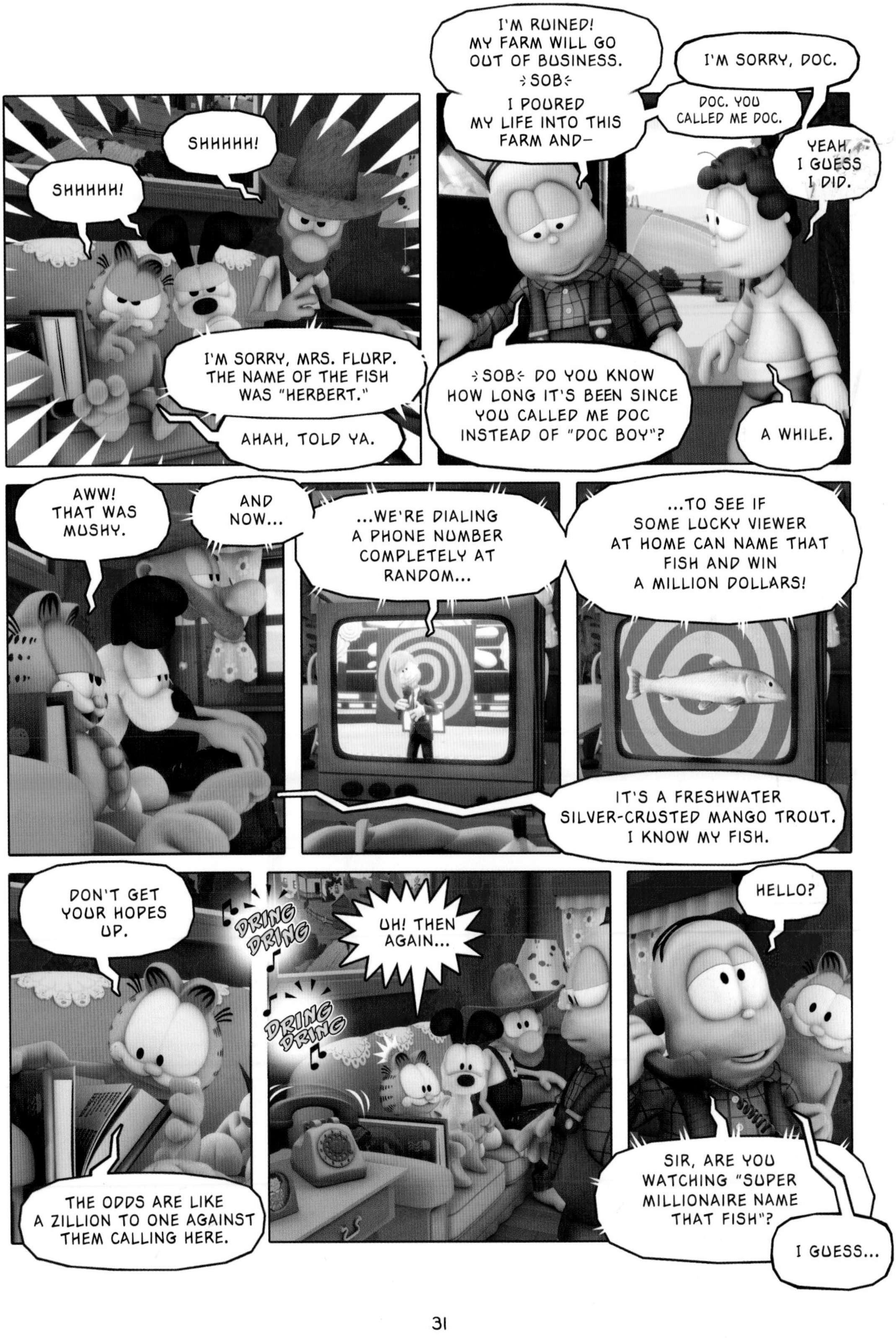
SHHHHH!
SHHHHH!
I'M SORRY, MRS. FLURP. THE NAME OF THE FISH WAS "HERBERT."
AHAH, TOLD YA.
I'M RUINED! MY FARM WILL GO OUT OF BUSINESS. ⁘SOB⁘
I POURED MY LIFE INTO THIS FARM AND–
I'M SORRY, DOC.
DOC. YOU CALLED ME DOC.
YEAH, I GUESS I DID.
⁘SOB⁘ DO YOU KNOW HOW LONG IT'S BEEN SINCE YOU CALLED ME DOC INSTEAD OF "DOC BOY"?
A WHILE.
AWW! THAT WAS MUSHY.
AND NOW...
...WE'RE DIALING A PHONE NUMBER COMPLETELY AT RANDOM...
...TO SEE IF SOME LUCKY VIEWER AT HOME CAN NAME THAT FISH AND WIN A MILLION DOLLARS!
IT'S A FRESHWATER SILVER-CRUSTED MANGO TROUT. I KNOW MY FISH.
DON'T GET YOUR HOPES UP.
THE ODDS ARE LIKE A ZILLION TO ONE AGAINST THEM CALLING HERE.
DRING DRING
UH! THEN AGAIN...
DRING DRING
HELLO?
SIR, ARE YOU WATCHING "SUPER MILLIONAIRE NAME THAT FISH"?
I GUESS...

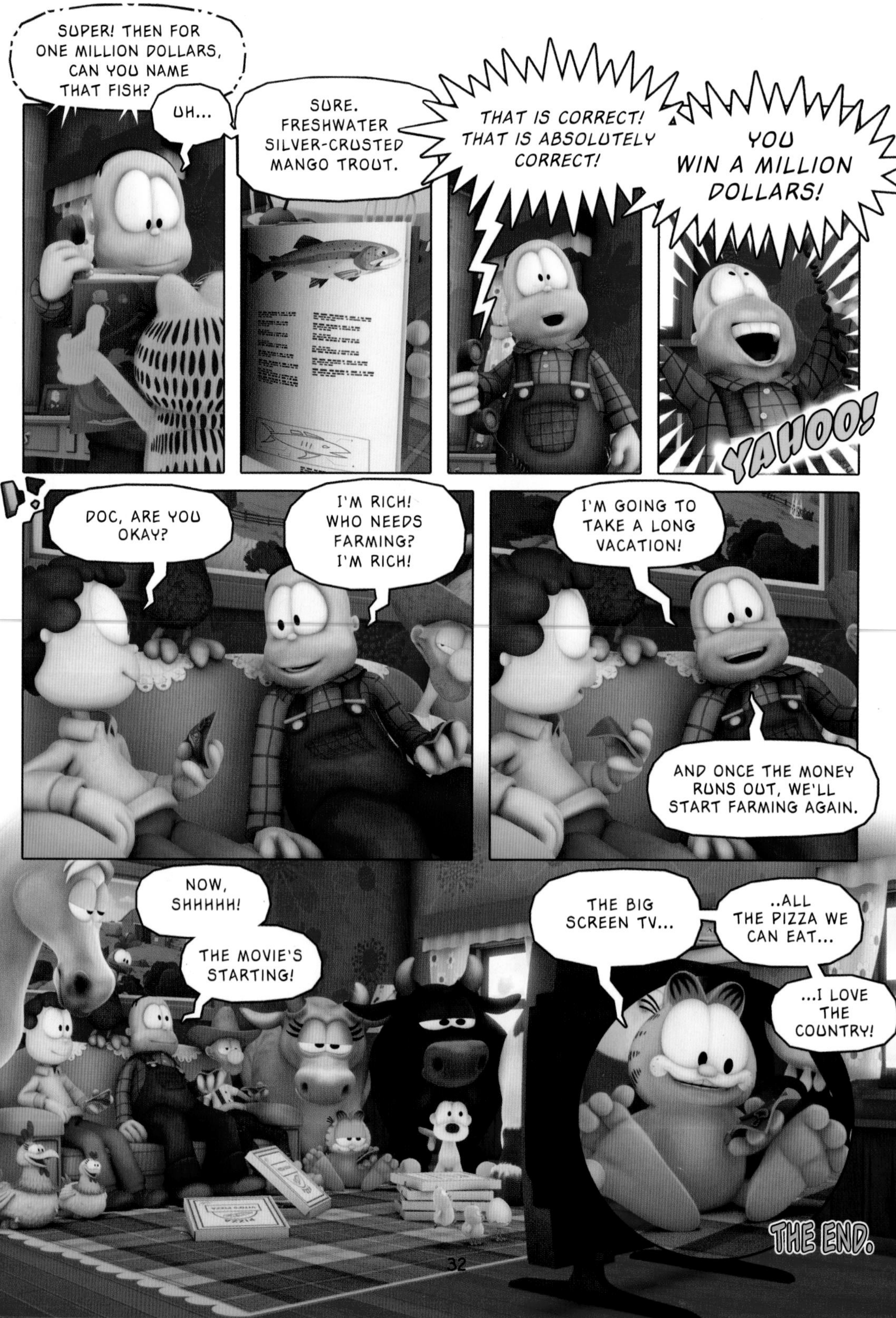
SUPER! THEN FOR ONE MILLION DOLLARS, CAN YOU NAME THAT FISH?
UH...
SURE. FRESHWATER SILVER-CRUSTED MANGO TROUT.
THAT IS CORRECT! THAT IS ABSOLUTELY CORRECT!
YOU WIN A MILLION DOLLARS!
YAHOO!
DOC, ARE YOU OKAY?
I'M RICH! WHO NEEDS FARMING? I'M RICH!
I'M GOING TO TAKE A LONG VACATION!
AND ONCE THE MONEY RUNS OUT, WE'LL START FARMING AGAIN.
NOW, SHHHHH!
THE MOVIE'S STARTING!
THE BIG SCREEN TV...
..ALL THE PIZZA WE CAN EAT...
...I LOVE THE COUNTRY!
THE END.

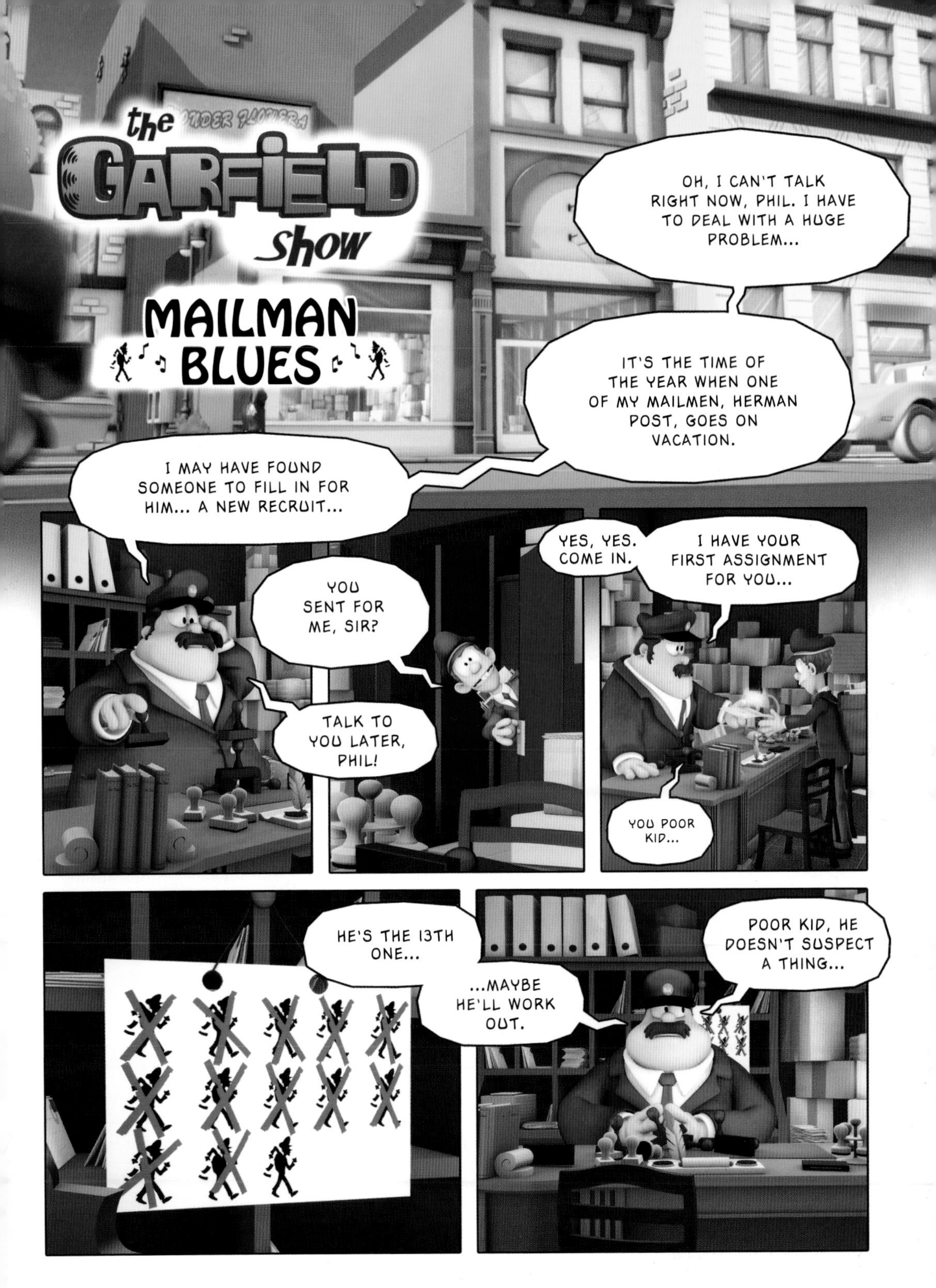
the GARFIELD show
MAILMAN BLUES
OH, I CAN'T TALK RIGHT NOW, PHIL. I HAVE TO DEAL WITH A HUGE PROBLEM...
IT'S THE TIME OF THE YEAR WHEN ONE OF MY MAILMEN, HERMAN POST, GOES ON VACATION.
I MAY HAVE FOUND SOMEONE TO FILL IN FOR HIM... A NEW RECRUIT...
YOU SENT FOR ME, SIR?
TALK TO YOU LATER, PHIL!
YES, YES. COME IN.
I HAVE YOUR FIRST ASSIGNMENT FOR YOU...
YOU POOR KID...
HE'S THE 13TH ONE...
...MAYBE HE'LL WORK OUT.
POOR KID, HE DOESN'T SUSPECT A THING...

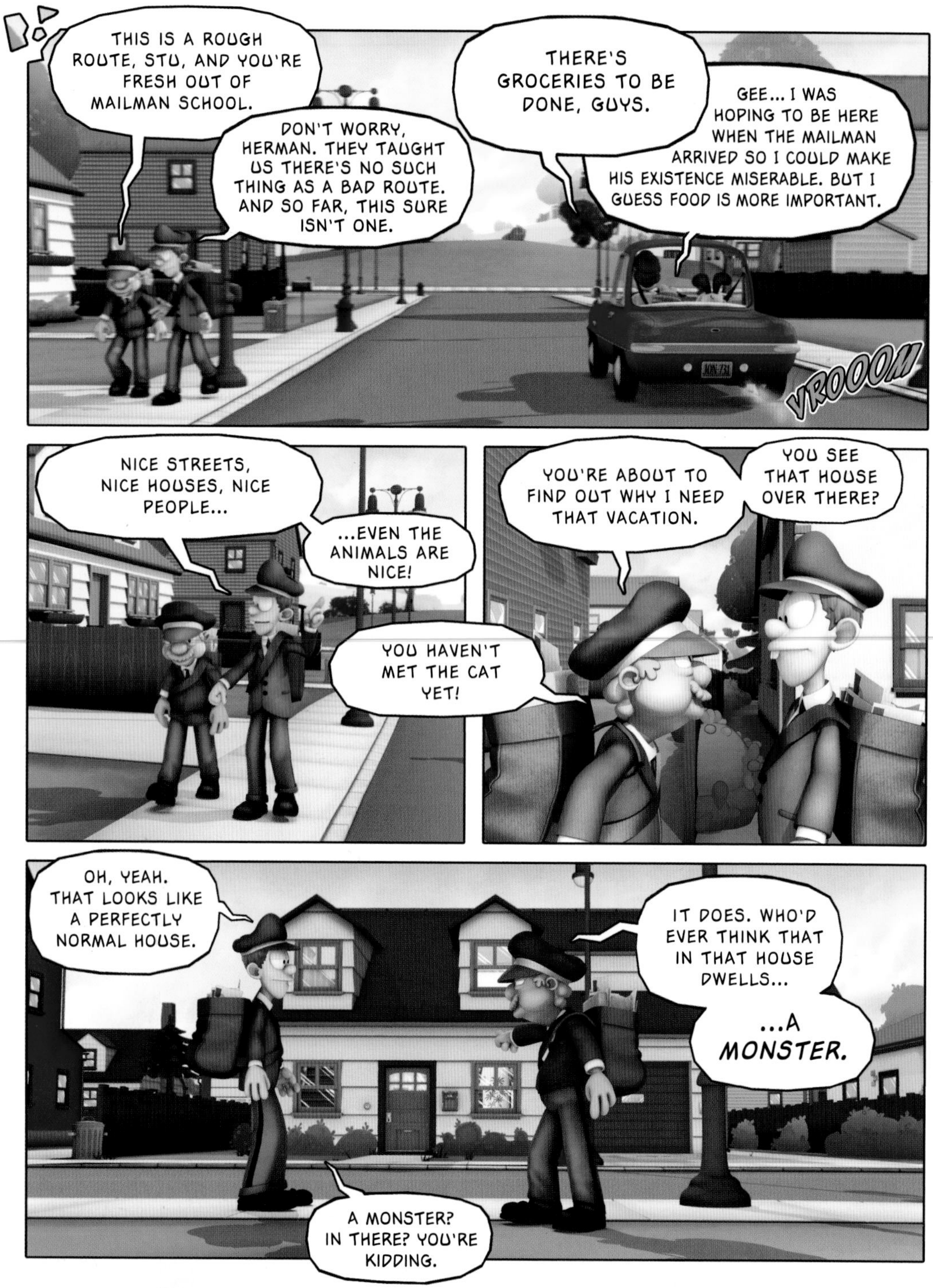

THIS IS A ROUGH ROUTE, STU, AND YOU'RE FRESH OUT OF MAILMAN SCHOOL.
DON'T WORRY, HERMAN. THEY TAUGHT US THERE'S NO SUCH THING AS A BAD ROUTE. AND SO FAR, THIS SURE ISN'T ONE.
THERE'S GROCERIES TO BE DONE, GUYS.
GEE... I WAS HOPING TO BE HERE WHEN THE MAILMAN ARRIVED SO I COULD MAKE HIS EXISTENCE MISERABLE. BUT I GUESS FOOD IS MORE IMPORTANT.
VROOOM
NICE STREETS, NICE HOUSES, NICE PEOPLE...
...EVEN THE ANIMALS ARE NICE!
YOU HAVEN'T MET THE CAT YET!
YOU'RE ABOUT TO FIND OUT WHY I NEED THAT VACATION.
YOU SEE THAT HOUSE OVER THERE?
OH, YEAH. THAT LOOKS LIKE A PERFECTLY NORMAL HOUSE.
IT DOES. WHO'D EVER THINK THAT IN THAT HOUSE DWELLS...
...A MONSTER.
A MONSTER? IN THERE? YOU'RE KIDDING.

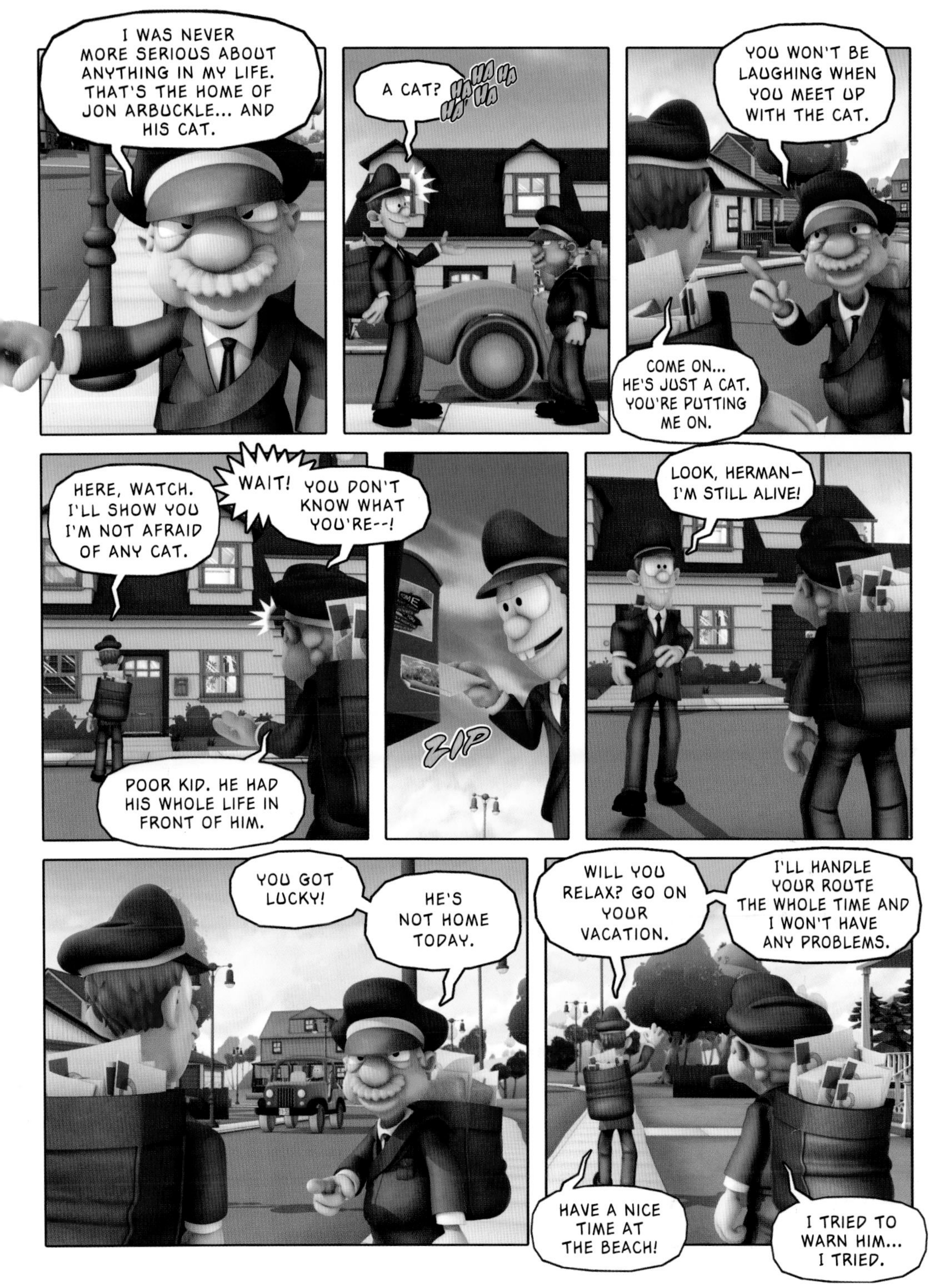
I WAS NEVER MORE SERIOUS ABOUT ANYTHING IN MY LIFE. THAT'S THE HOME OF JON ARBUCKLE... AND HIS CAT.
A CAT?
HA HA HA HA HA
YOU WON'T BE LAUGHING WHEN YOU MEET UP WITH THE CAT.
COME ON... HE'S JUST A CAT. YOU'RE PUTTING ME ON.
HERE, WATCH. I'LL SHOW YOU I'M NOT AFRAID OF ANY CAT.
WAIT!
YOU DON'T KNOW WHAT YOU'RE--!
POOR KID. HE HAD HIS WHOLE LIFE IN FRONT OF HIM.
ZIP
LOOK, HERMAN— I'M STILL ALIVE!
YOU GOT LUCKY!
HE'S NOT HOME TODAY.
WILL YOU RELAX? GO ON YOUR VACATION.
I'LL HANDLE YOUR ROUTE THE WHOLE TIME AND I WON'T HAVE ANY PROBLEMS.
HAVE A NICE TIME AT THE BEACH!
I TRIED TO WARN HIM... I TRIED.

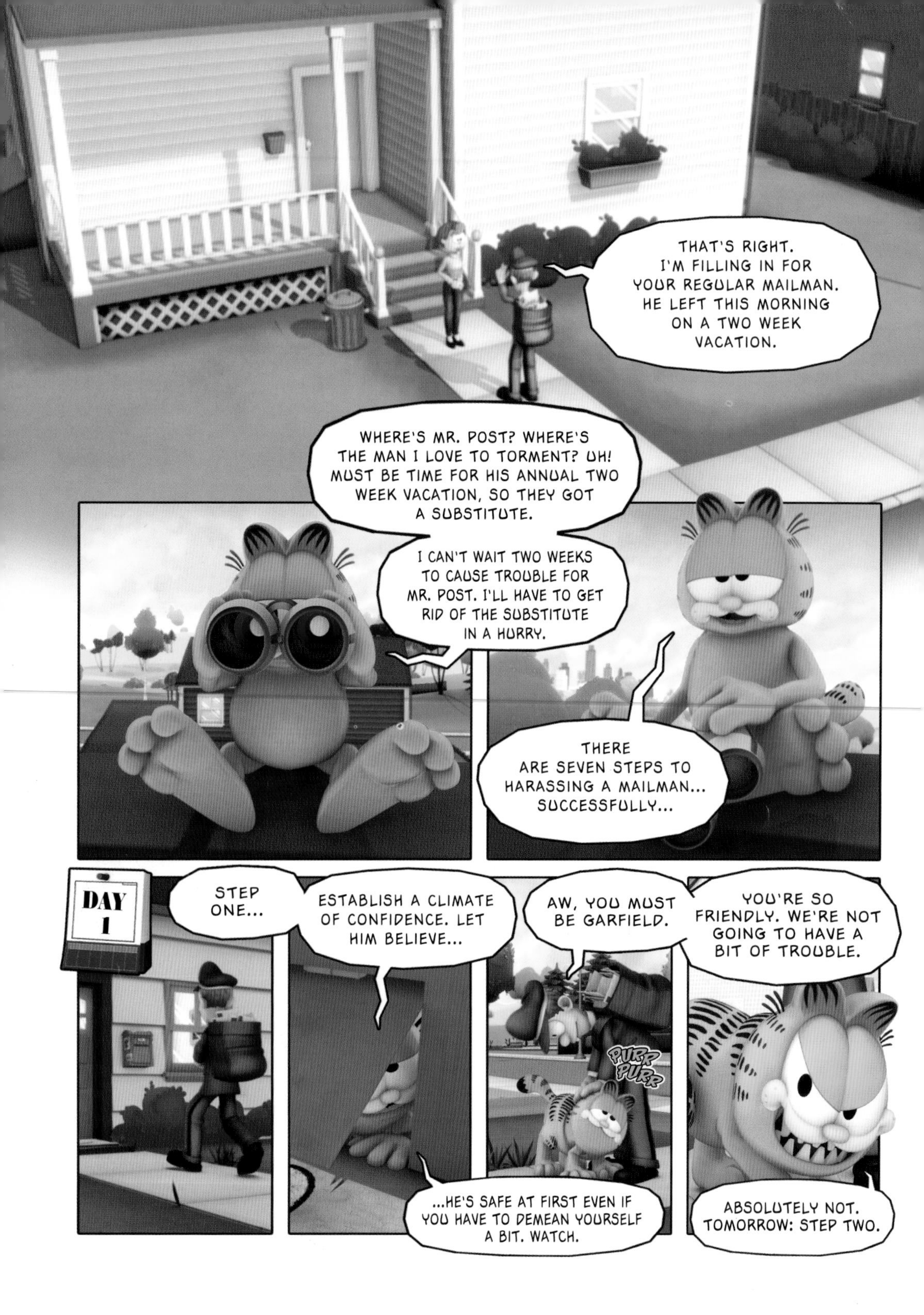
THAT'S RIGHT. I'M FILLING IN FOR YOUR REGULAR MAILMAN. HE LEFT THIS MORNING ON A TWO WEEK VACATION.
WHERE'S MR. POST? WHERE'S THE MAN I LOVE TO TORMENT? UH! MUST BE TIME FOR HIS ANNUAL TWO WEEK VACATION, SO THEY GOT A SUBSTITUTE.
I CAN'T WAIT TWO WEEKS TO CAUSE TROUBLE FOR MR. POST. I'LL HAVE TO GET RID OF THE SUBSTITUTE IN A HURRY.
THERE ARE SEVEN STEPS TO HARASSING A MAILMAN... SUCCESSFULLY...
DAY 1
STEP ONE...
ESTABLISH A CLIMATE OF CONFIDENCE. LET HIM BELIEVE...
...HE'S SAFE AT FIRST EVEN IF YOU HAVE TO DEMEAN YOURSELF A BIT. WATCH.
AW, YOU MUST BE GARFIELD.
PURR PURR
YOU'RE SO FRIENDLY. WE'RE NOT GOING TO HAVE A BIT OF TROUBLE.
ABSOLUTELY NOT. TOMORROW: STEP TWO.

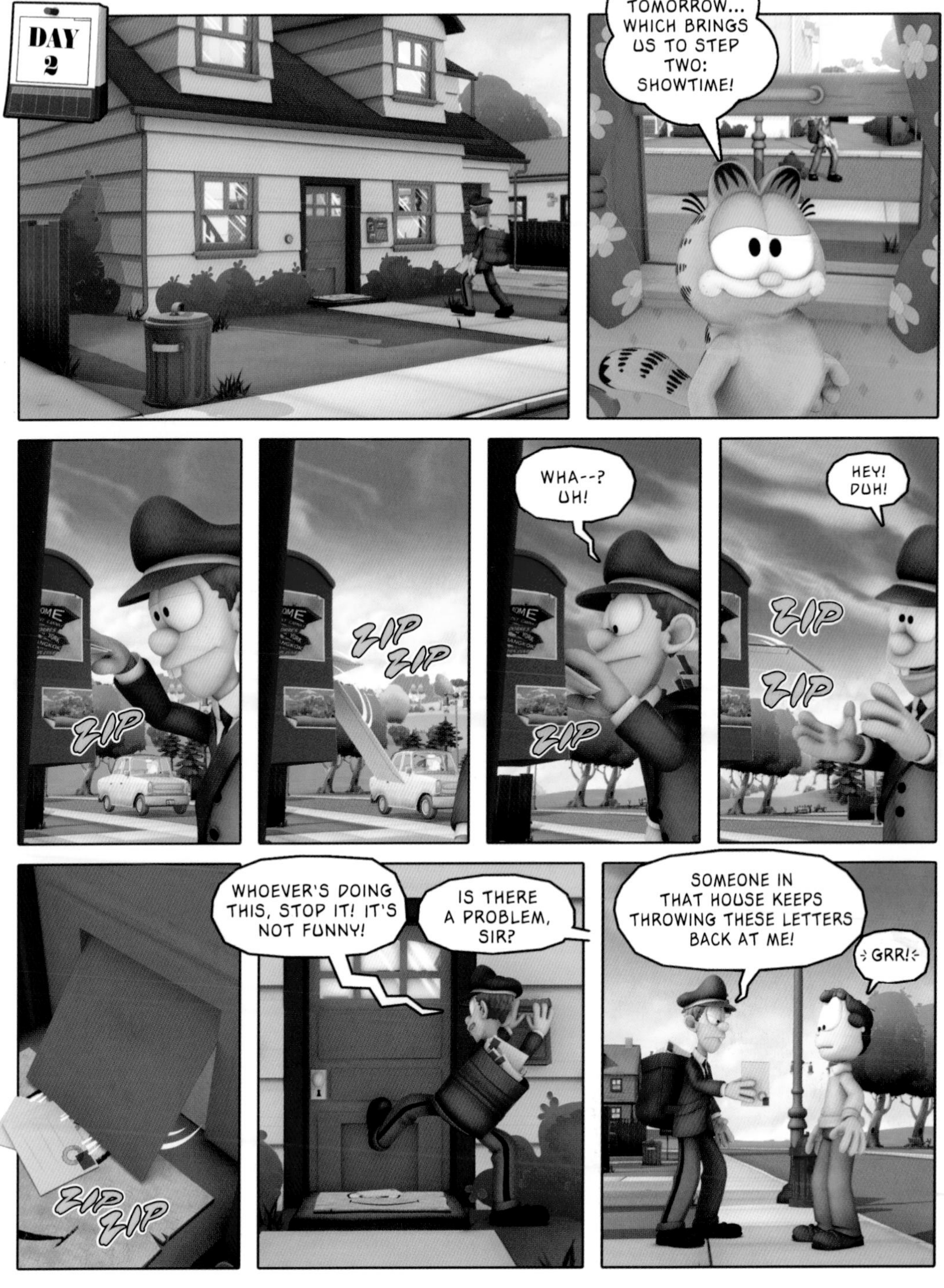
DAY 2
OKAY, IT'S TOMORROW... WHICH BRINGS US TO STEP TWO: SHOWTIME!
ZIP
ZIP
ZIP
WHA--? UH!
ZIP
HEY! DUH!
ZIP
ZIP
ZIP ZIP
WHOEVER'S DOING THIS, STOP IT! IT'S NOT FUNNY!
IS THERE A PROBLEM, SIR?
SOMEONE IN THAT HOUSE KEEPS THROWING THESE LETTERS BACK AT ME!
GRR!

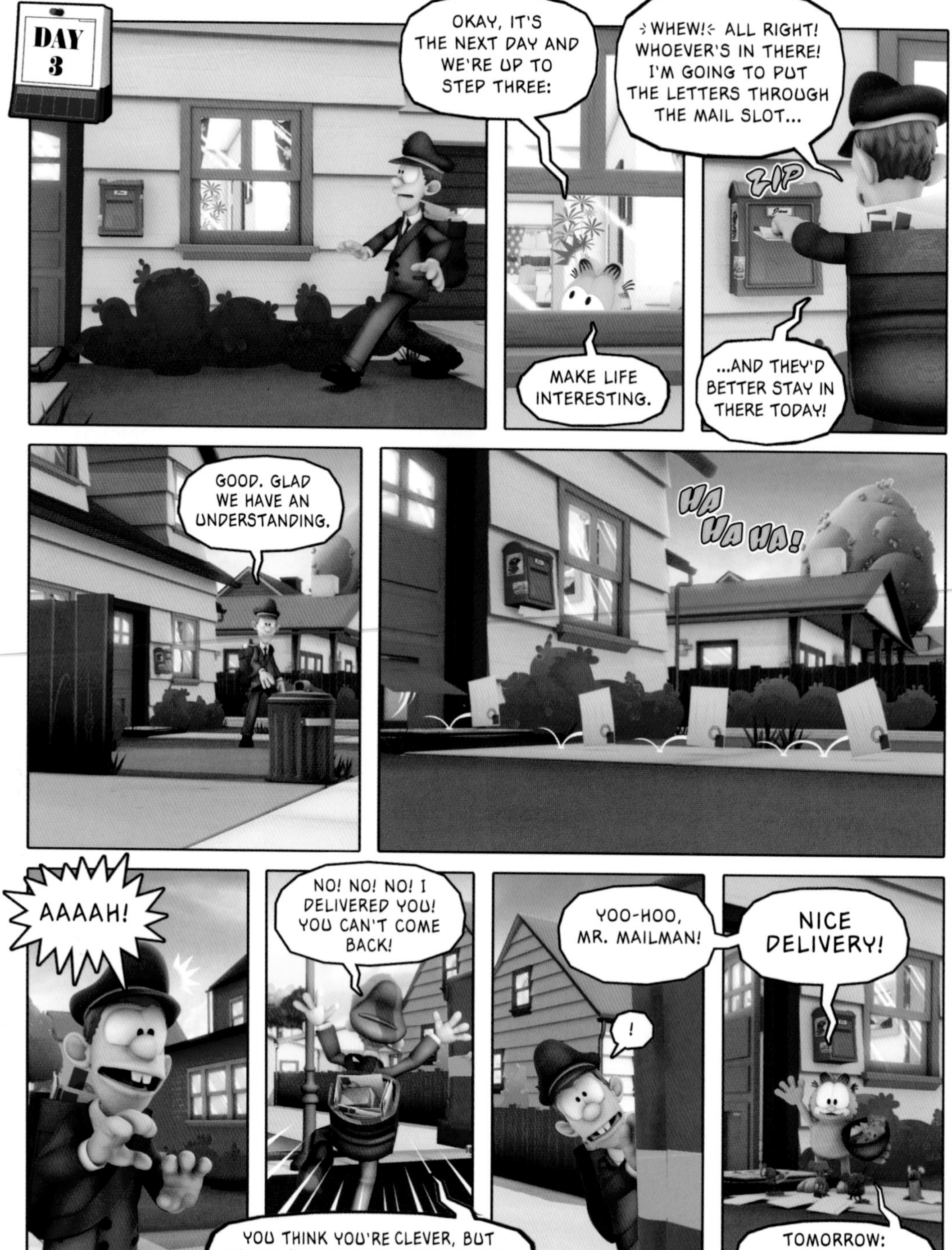

DAY 3
OKAY, IT'S THE NEXT DAY AND WE'RE UP TO STEP THREE:
MAKE LIFE INTERESTING.
→WHEW!← ALL RIGHT! WHOEVER'S IN THERE! I'M GOING TO PUT THE LETTERS THROUGH THE MAIL SLOT...
ZIP
...AND THEY'D BETTER STAY IN THERE TODAY!
GOOD. GLAD WE HAVE AN UNDERSTANDING.
HA HA HA HA!
AAAAH!
NO! NO! NO! I DELIVERED YOU! YOU CAN'T COME BACK!
YOU THINK YOU'RE CLEVER, BUT YOU'LL SEE. YOU PICKED THE WRONG MAILMAN TO MESS WITH!
YOO-HOO, MR. MAILMAN!
NICE DELIVERY!
!
TOMORROW: THE ALL-IMPORTANT STEP FOUR.

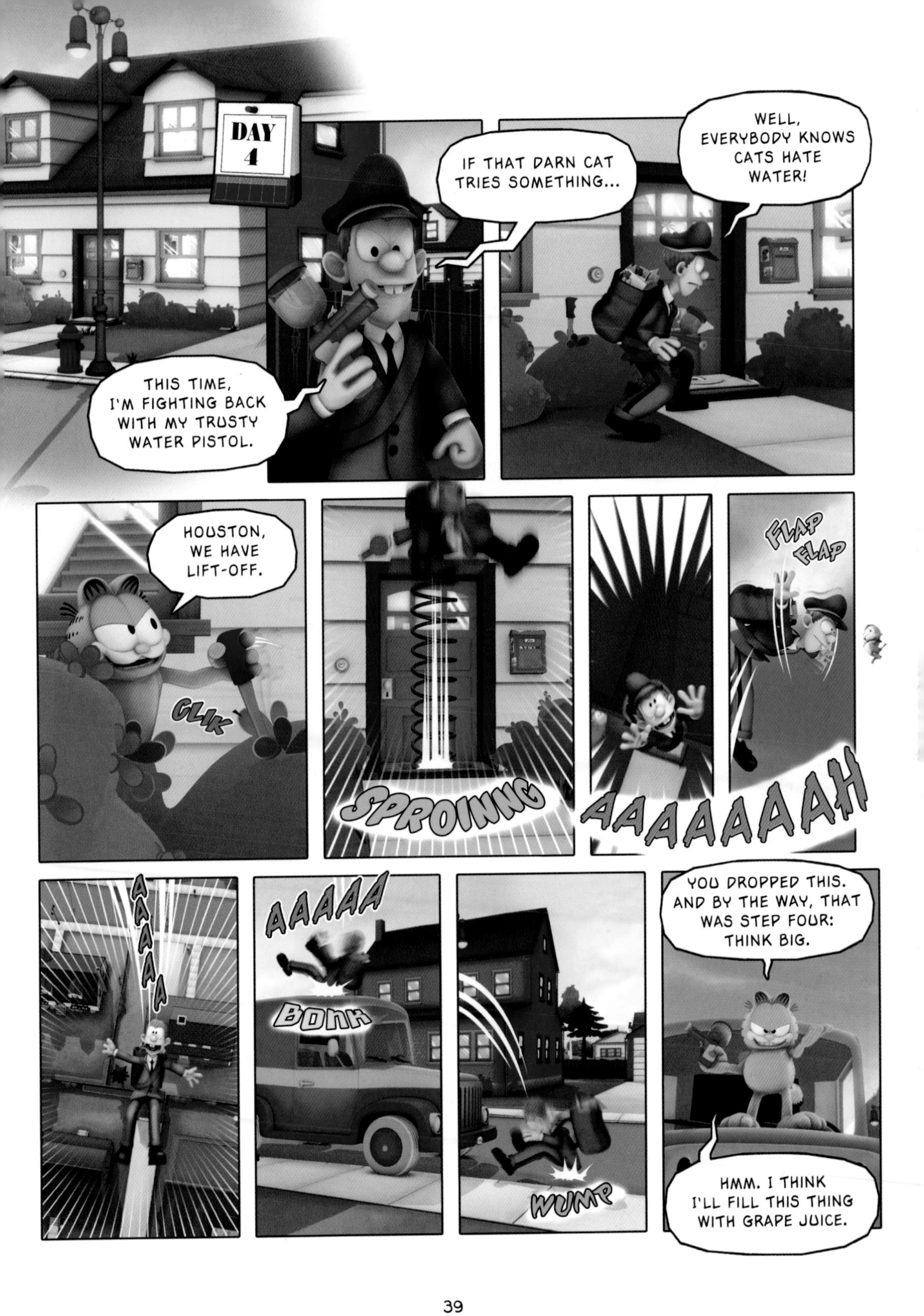
DAY 4
IF THAT DARN CAT TRIES SOMETHING...
THIS TIME, I'M FIGHTING BACK WITH MY TRUSTY WATER PISTOL.
WELL, EVERYBODY KNOWS CATS HATE WATER!
HOUSTON, WE HAVE LIFT-OFF.
CLIK
SPROINNG
FLAP FLAP
AAAAAAAAH
AAAAA
AAAAA
BONK
WUMP
YOU DROPPED THIS. AND BY THE WAY, THAT WAS STEP FOUR: THINK BIG.
HMM. I THINK I'LL FILL THIS THING WITH GRAPE JUICE.

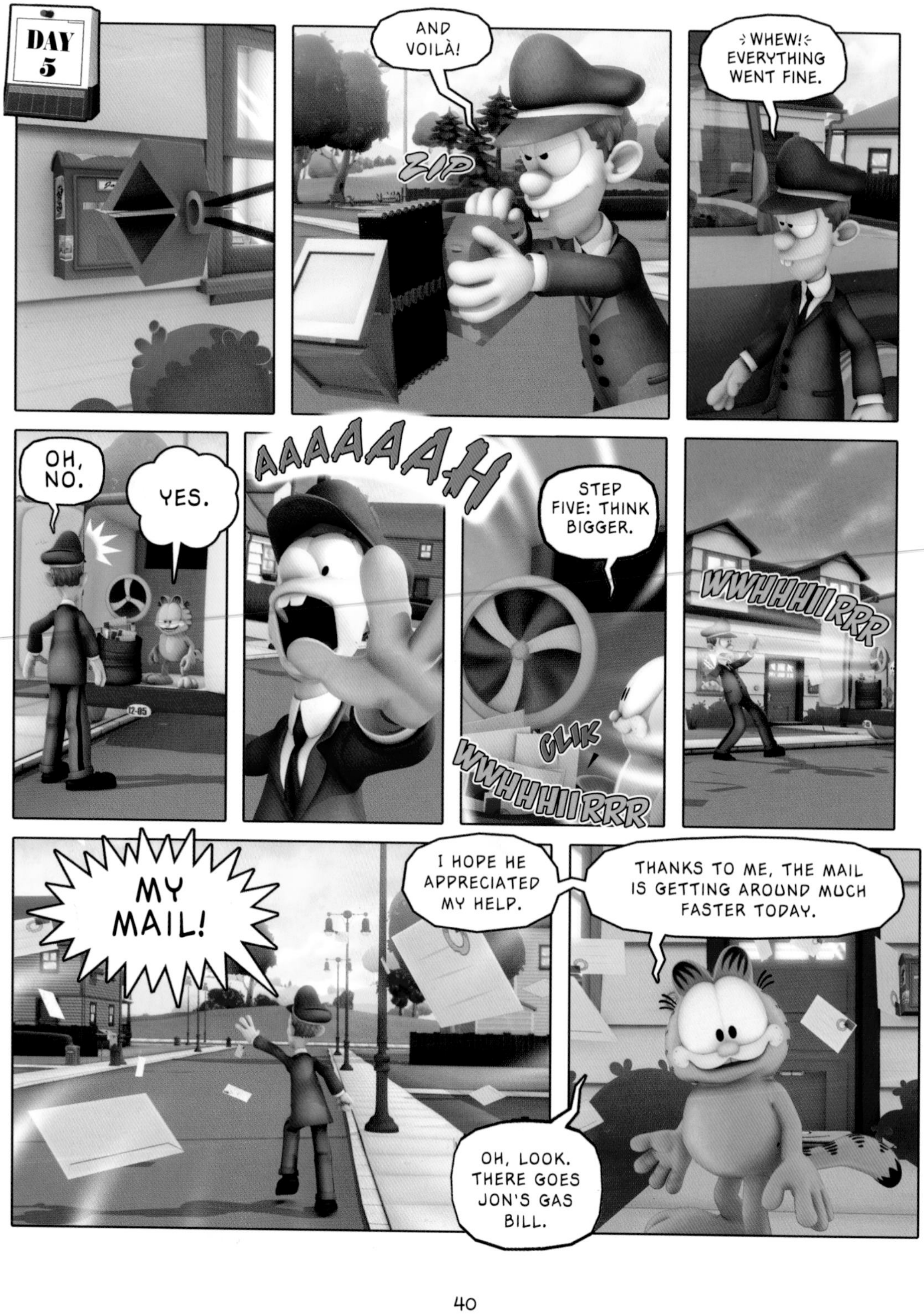
DAY 5
AND VOILÀ!
ZIP
WHEW! EVERYTHING WENT FINE.
OH, NO.
YES.
AAAAAAH
STEP FIVE: THINK BIGGER.
CLIK
WWHHHIIRRR
WWHHHIIRRR
MY MAIL!
I HOPE HE APPRECIATED MY HELP.
THANKS TO ME, THE MAIL IS GETTING AROUND MUCH FASTER TODAY.
OH, LOOK. THERE GOES JON'S GAS BILL.

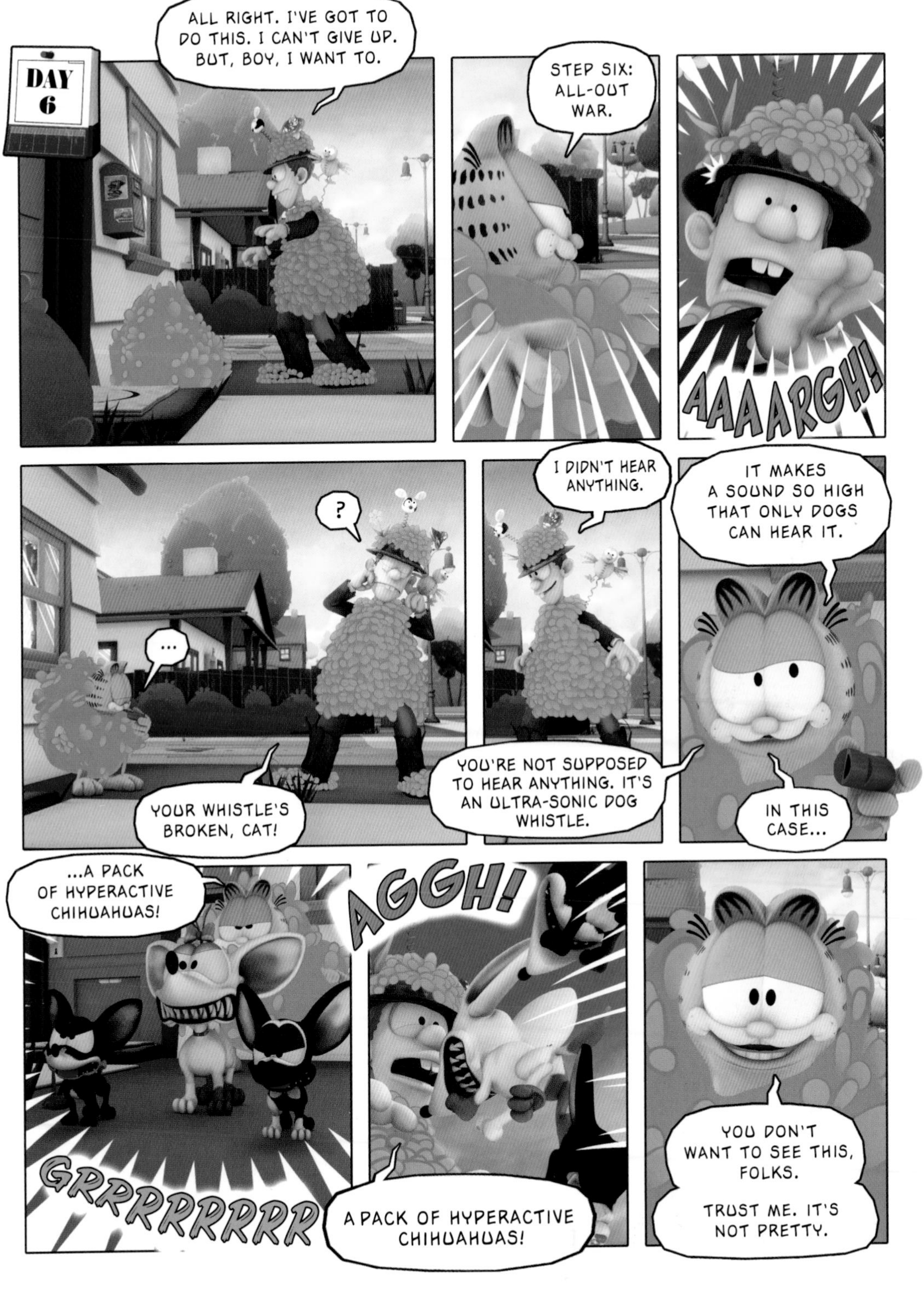
DAY 6
ALL RIGHT. I'VE GOT TO DO THIS. I CAN'T GIVE UP. BUT, BOY, I WANT TO.
STEP SIX: ALL-OUT WAR.
AAAARGH!
?
...
I DIDN'T HEAR ANYTHING.
YOUR WHISTLE'S BROKEN, CAT!
YOU'RE NOT SUPPOSED TO HEAR ANYTHING. IT'S AN ULTRA-SONIC DOG WHISTLE.
IT MAKES A SOUND SO HIGH THAT ONLY DOGS CAN HEAR IT.
IN THIS CASE...
...A PACK OF HYPERACTIVE CHIHUAHUAS!
GRRRRRRRRR
AGGH!
A PACK OF HYPERACTIVE CHIHUAHUAS!
YOU DON'T WANT TO SEE THIS, FOLKS.
TRUST ME. IT'S NOT PRETTY.

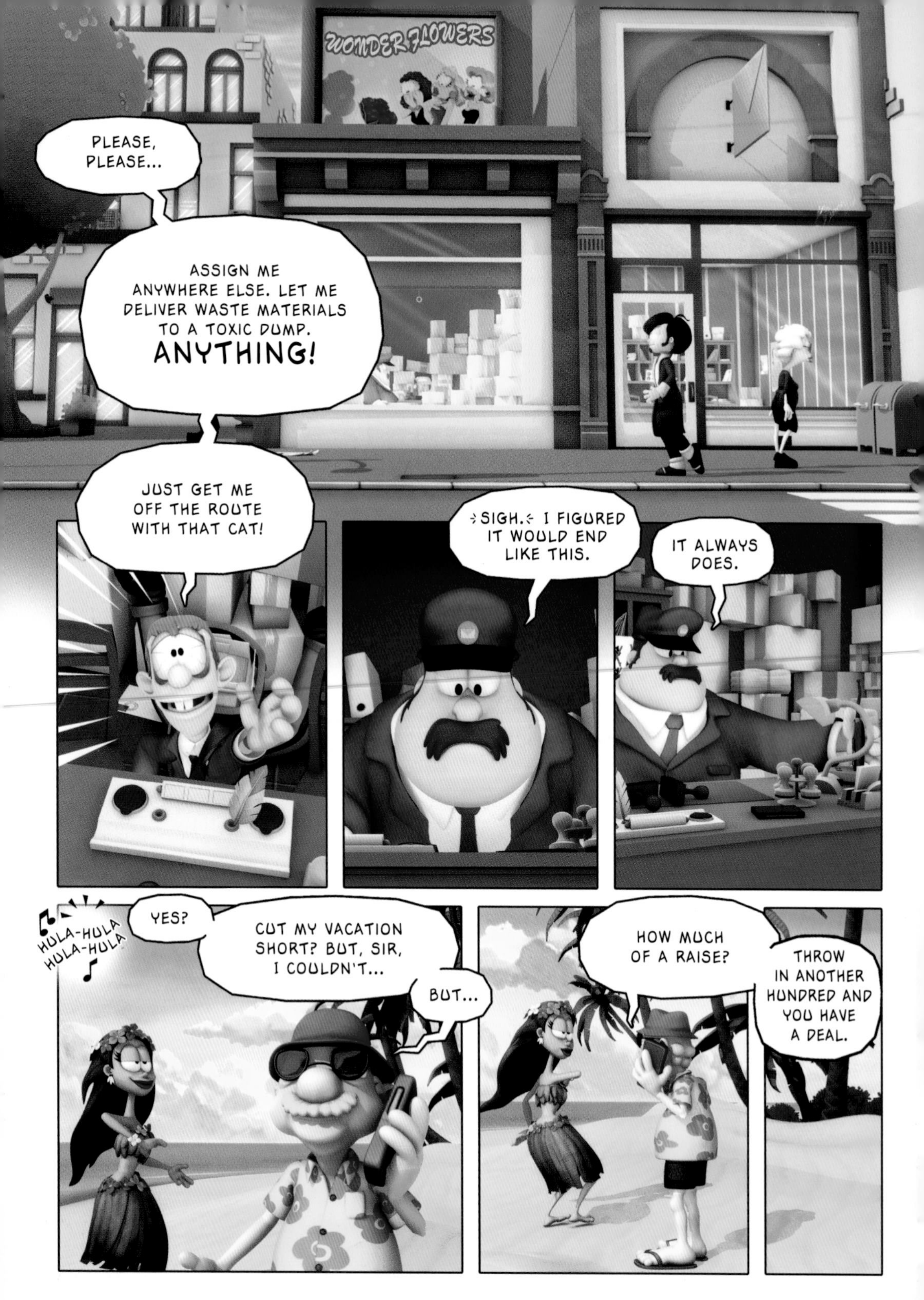
WONDER FLOWERS
PLEASE, PLEASE...
ASSIGN ME ANYWHERE ELSE. LET ME DELIVER WASTE MATERIALS TO A TOXIC DUMP. ANYTHING!
JUST GET ME OFF THE ROUTE WITH THAT CAT!
SIGH. I FIGURED IT WOULD END LIKE THIS.
IT ALWAYS DOES.
HULA-HULA HULA-HULA
YES?
CUT MY VACATION SHORT? BUT, SIR, I COULDN'T...
BUT...
HOW MUCH OF A RAISE?
THROW IN ANOTHER HUNDRED AND YOU HAVE A DEAL.

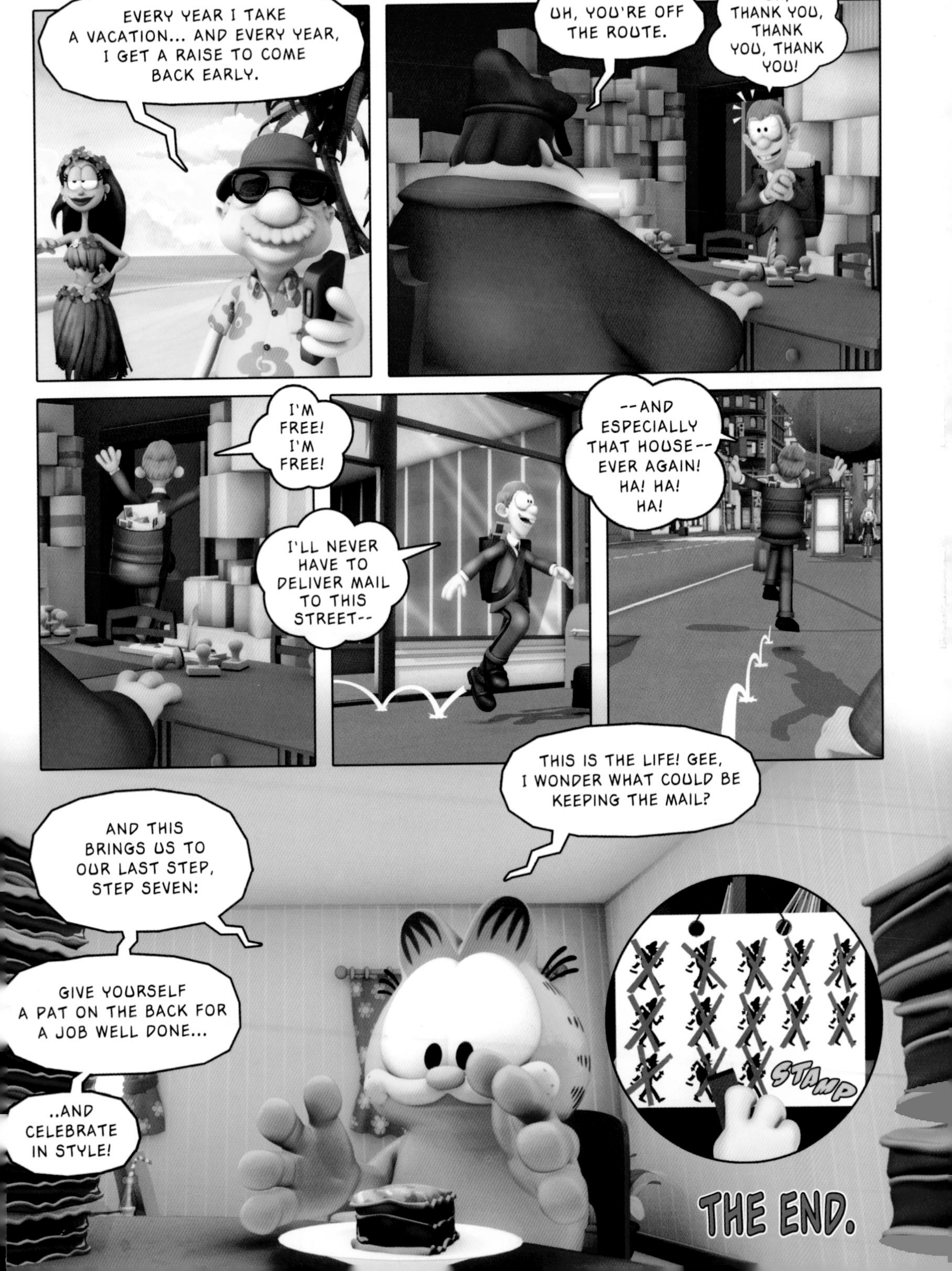
EVERY YEAR I TAKE A VACATION... AND EVERY YEAR, I GET A RAISE TO COME BACK EARLY.
UH, YOU'RE OFF THE ROUTE.
OH, THANK YOU, THANK YOU, THANK YOU!
I'M FREE! I'M FREE!
I'LL NEVER HAVE TO DELIVER MAIL TO THIS STREET--
--AND ESPECIALLY THAT HOUSE-- EVER AGAIN! HA! HA! HA!
THIS IS THE LIFE! GEE, I WONDER WHAT COULD BE KEEPING THE MAIL?
AND THIS BRINGS US TO OUR LAST STEP, STEP SEVEN:
GIVE YOURSELF A PAT ON THE BACK FOR A JOB WELL DONE...
..AND CELEBRATE IN STYLE!
STAMP
THE END.

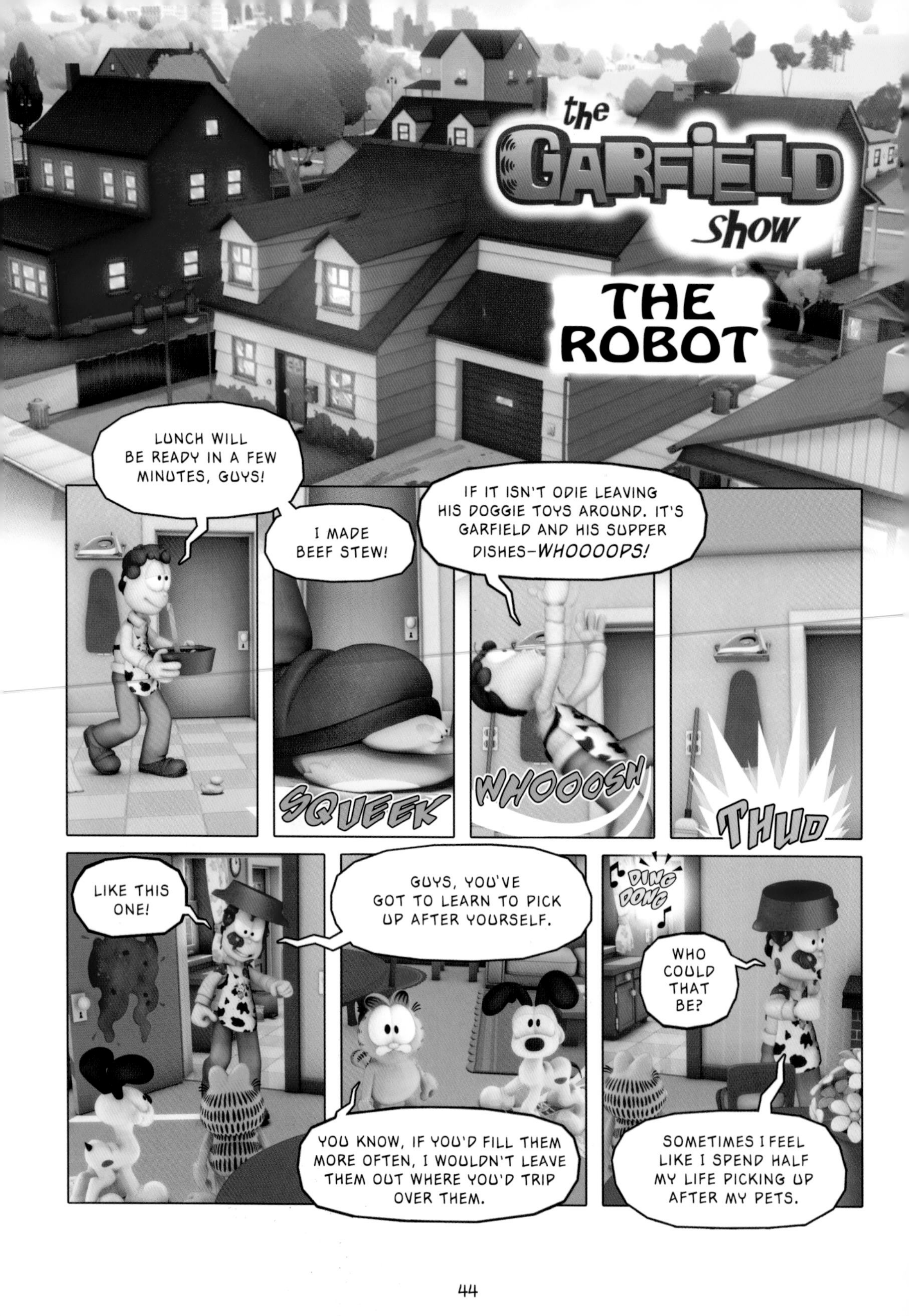
the GARFIELD show
THE ROBOT
LUNCH WILL BE READY IN A FEW MINUTES, GUYS!
I MADE BEEF STEW!
SQUEEK
IF IT ISN'T ODIE LEAVING HIS DOGGIE TOYS AROUND. IT'S GARFIELD AND HIS SUPPER DISHES–WHOOOOPS!
WHOOOOSH
THUD
LIKE THIS ONE!
GUYS, YOU'VE GOT TO LEARN TO PICK UP AFTER YOURSELF.
YOU KNOW, IF YOU'D FILL THEM MORE OFTEN, I WOULDN'T LEAVE THEM OUT WHERE YOU'D TRIP OVER THEM.
DING DONG
WHO COULD THAT BE?
SOMETIMES I FEEL LIKE I SPEND HALF MY LIFE PICKING UP AFTER MY PETS.

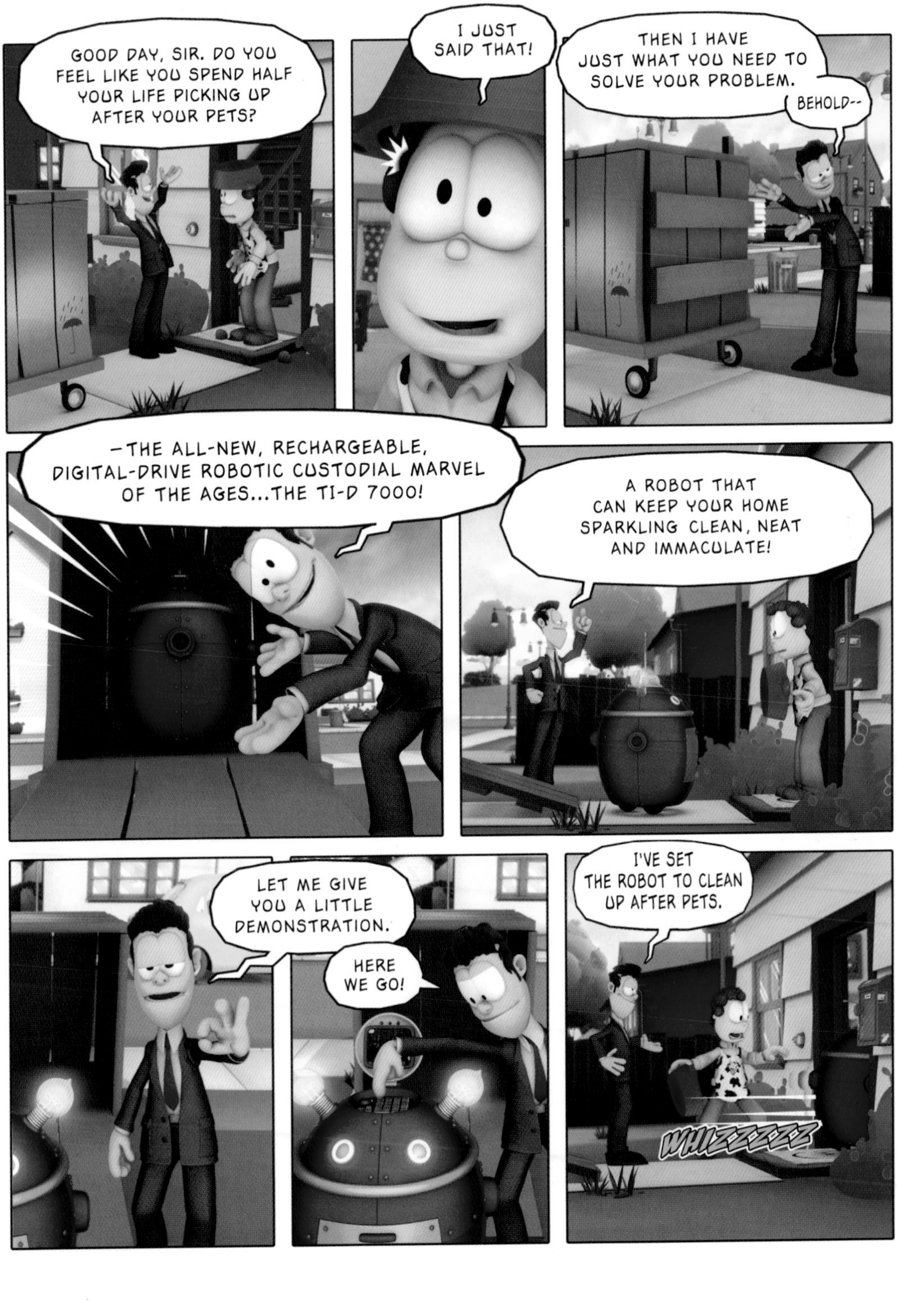
GOOD DAY, SIR. DO YOU FEEL LIKE YOU SPEND HALF YOUR LIFE PICKING UP AFTER YOUR PETS?
I JUST SAID THAT!
THEN I HAVE JUST WHAT YOU NEED TO SOLVE YOUR PROBLEM.
BEHOLD--
-THE ALL-NEW, RECHARGEABLE, DIGITAL-DRIVE ROBOTIC CUSTODIAL MARVEL OF THE AGES...THE TI-D 7000!
A ROBOT THAT CAN KEEP YOUR HOME SPARKLING CLEAN, NEAT AND IMMACULATE!
LET ME GIVE YOU A LITTLE DEMONSTRATION.
HERE WE GO!
I'VE SET THE ROBOT TO CLEAN UP AFTER PETS.
WHIZZZZZ

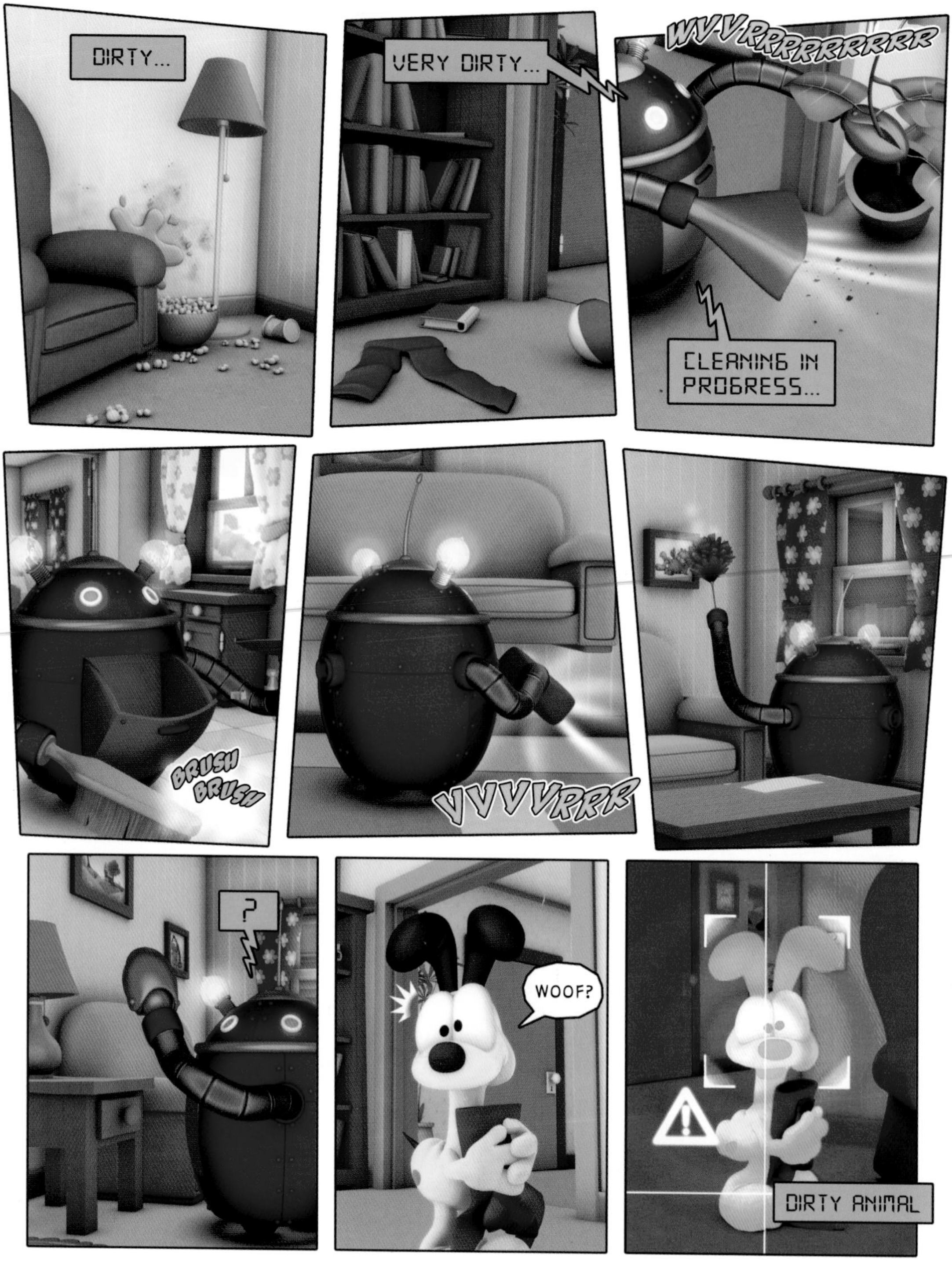
DIRTY...
VERY DIRTY...
WVVVRRRRRRRRRR
CLEANING IN PROGRESS...
BRUSH BRUSH
VVVVRRRR
?
WOOF?
DIRTY ANIMAL

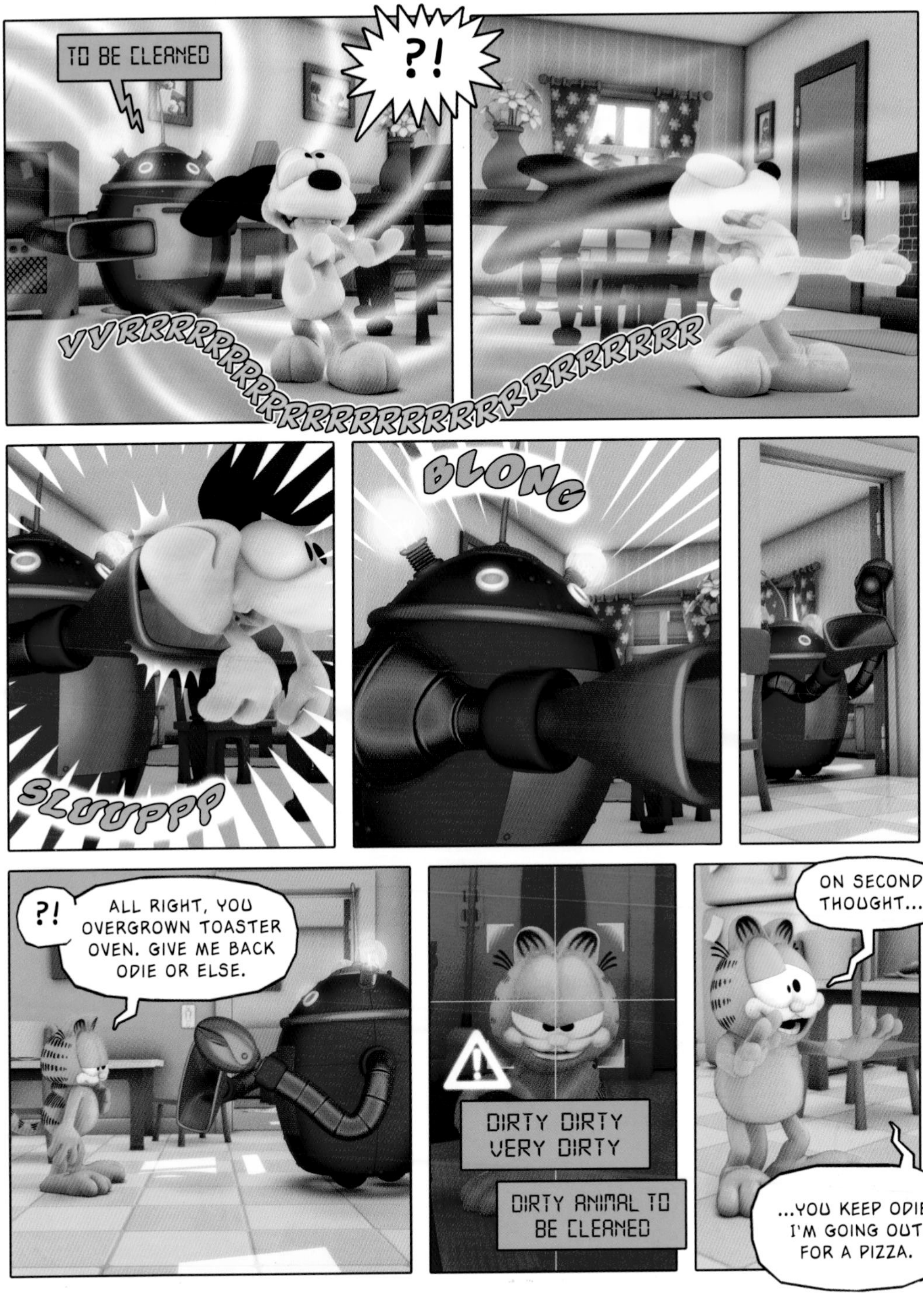
TO BE CLEANED
?!
VVRRRRRRRRRRRRRRRRRRRRRRRRRRRRRRRRR
SLUUPPP
BLONG
?!
ALL RIGHT, YOU OVERGROWN TOASTER OVEN. GIVE ME BACK ODIE OR ELSE.
DIRTY DIRTY VERY DIRTY
DIRTY ANIMAL TO BE CLEANED
ON SECOND THOUGHT...
...YOU KEEP ODIE. I'M GOING OUT FOR A PIZZA.

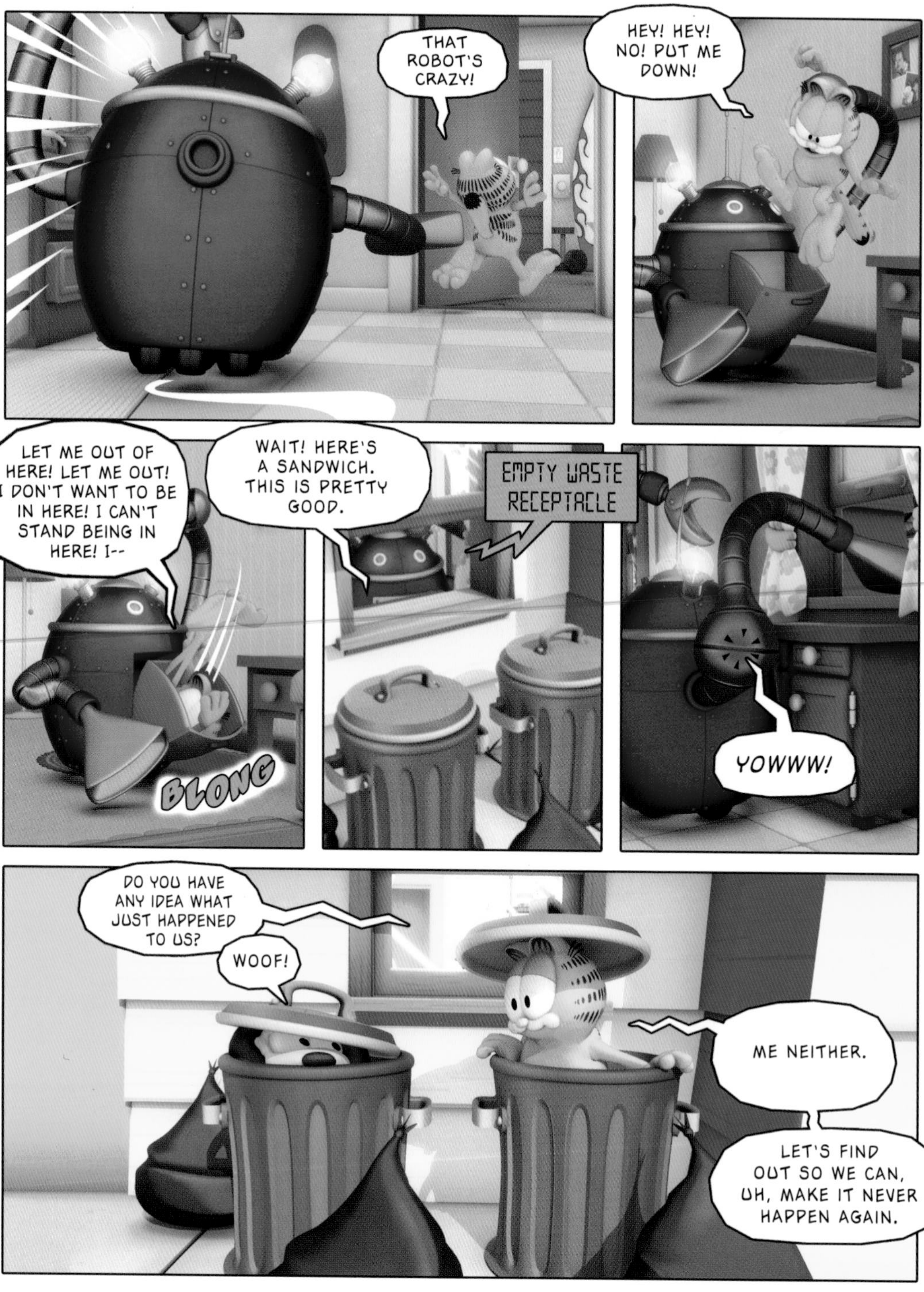
THAT ROBOT'S CRAZY!
HEY! HEY! NO! PUT ME DOWN!
LET ME OUT OF HERE! LET ME OUT! I DON'T WANT TO BE IN HERE! I CAN'T STAND BEING IN HERE! I--
BLONG
WAIT! HERE'S A SANDWICH. THIS IS PRETTY GOOD.
EMPTY WASTE RECEPTACLE
YOWWW!
DO YOU HAVE ANY IDEA WHAT JUST HAPPENED TO US?
WOOF!
ME NEITHER.
LET'S FIND OUT SO WE CAN, UH, MAKE IT NEVER HAPPEN AGAIN.

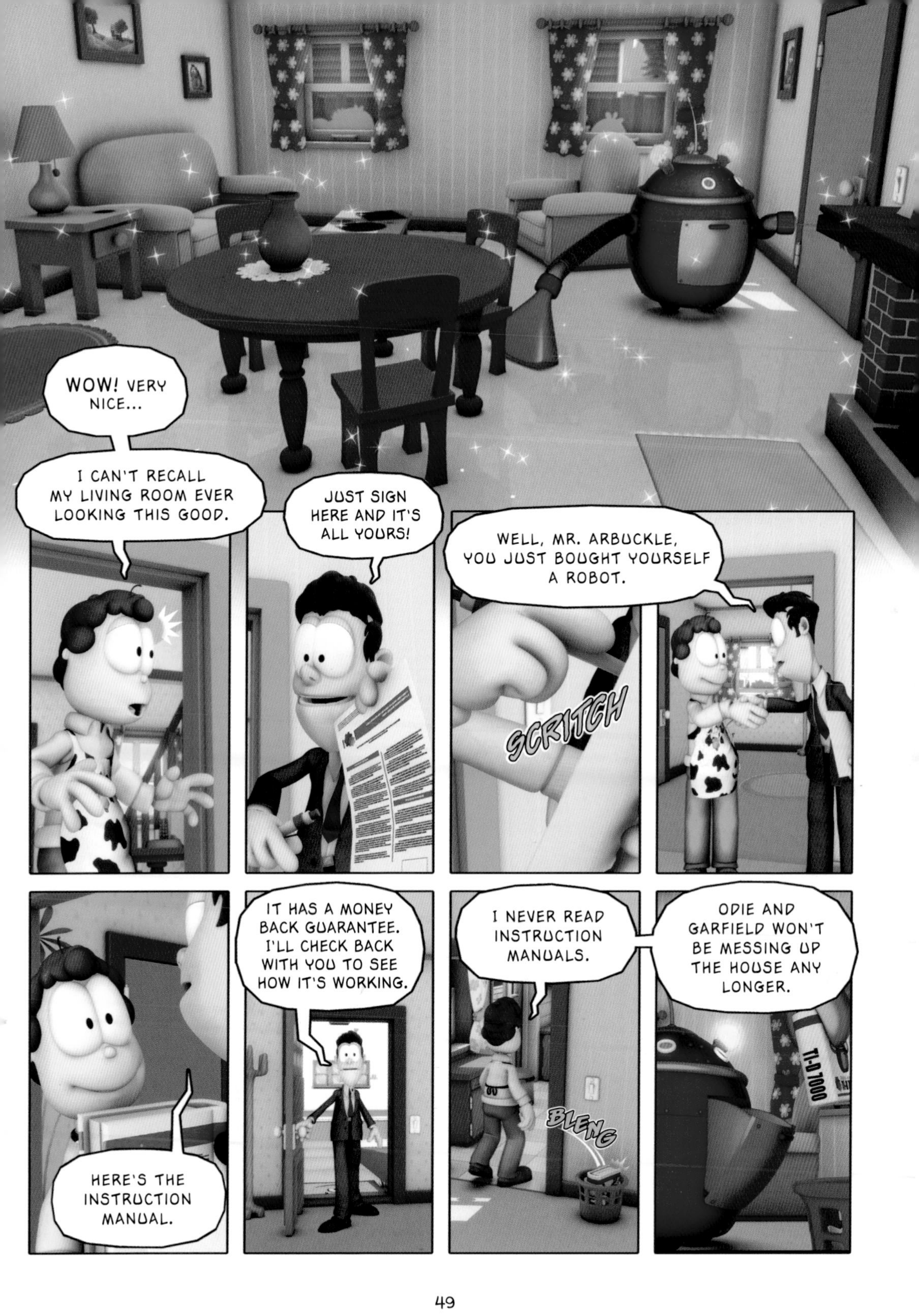
WOW! VERY NICE...
I CAN'T RECALL MY LIVING ROOM EVER LOOKING THIS GOOD.
JUST SIGN HERE AND IT'S ALL YOURS!
SCRITCH
WELL, MR. ARBUCKLE, YOU JUST BOUGHT YOURSELF A ROBOT.
HERE'S THE INSTRUCTION MANUAL.
IT HAS A MONEY BACK GUARANTEE. I'LL CHECK BACK WITH YOU TO SEE HOW IT'S WORKING.
I NEVER READ INSTRUCTION MANUALS.
BLENG
ODIE AND GARFIELD WON'T BE MESSING UP THE HOUSE ANY LONGER.
TI-D 7000

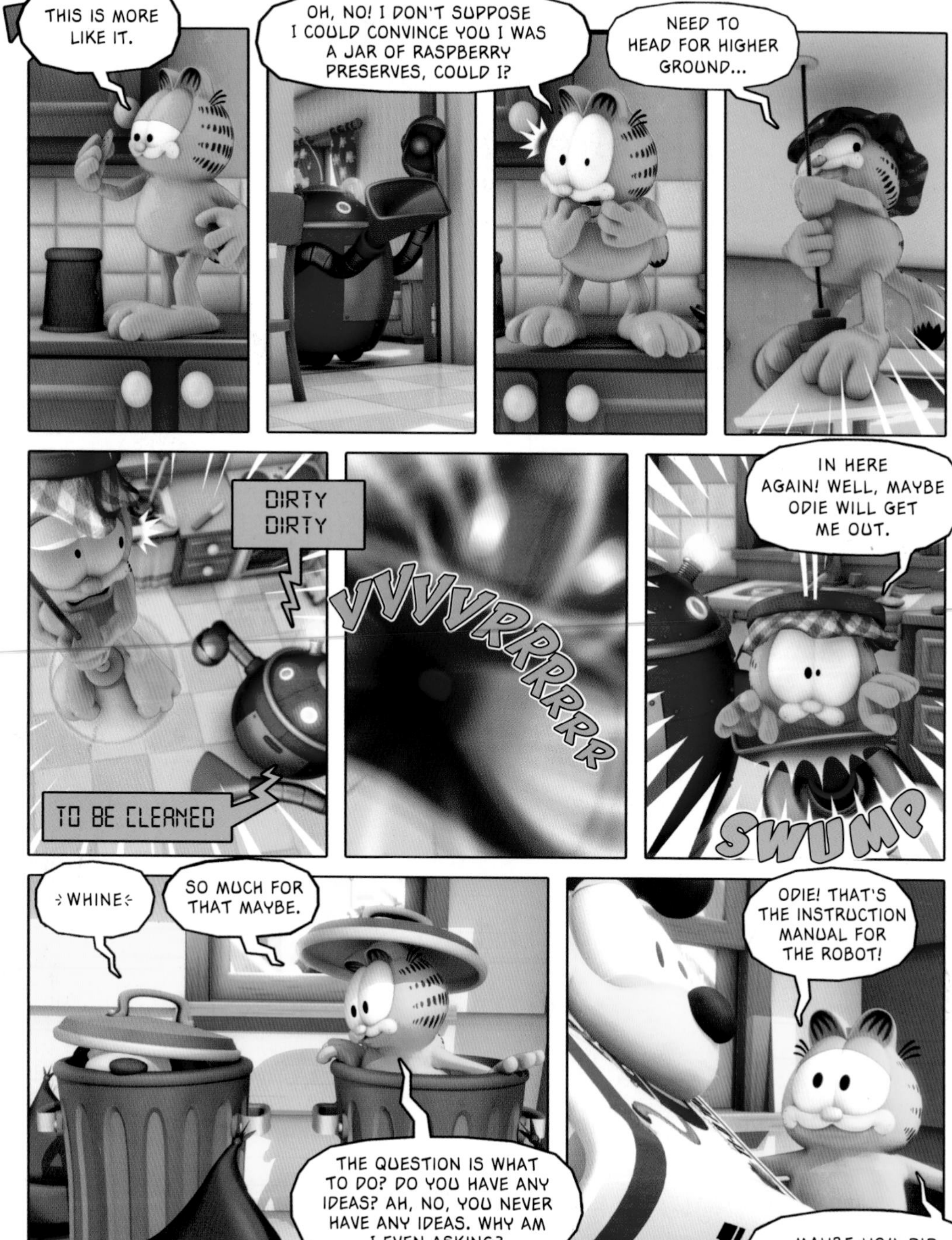
THIS IS MORE LIKE IT.
OH, NO! I DON'T SUPPOSE I COULD CONVINCE YOU I WAS A JAR OF RASPBERRY PRESERVES, COULD I?
NEED TO HEAD FOR HIGHER GROUND...
DIRTY DIRTY
TO BE CLEANED
VVVVRRRRRRR
IN HERE AGAIN! WELL, MAYBE ODIE WILL GET ME OUT.
SWUMP
WHINE
SO MUCH FOR THAT MAYBE.
THE QUESTION IS WHAT TO DO? DO YOU HAVE ANY IDEAS? AH, NO, YOU NEVER HAVE ANY IDEAS. WHY AM I EVEN ASKING?
ODIE! THAT'S THE INSTRUCTION MANUAL FOR THE ROBOT!
MAYBE YOU DID HAVE AN IDEA AND DIDN'T KNOW IT.

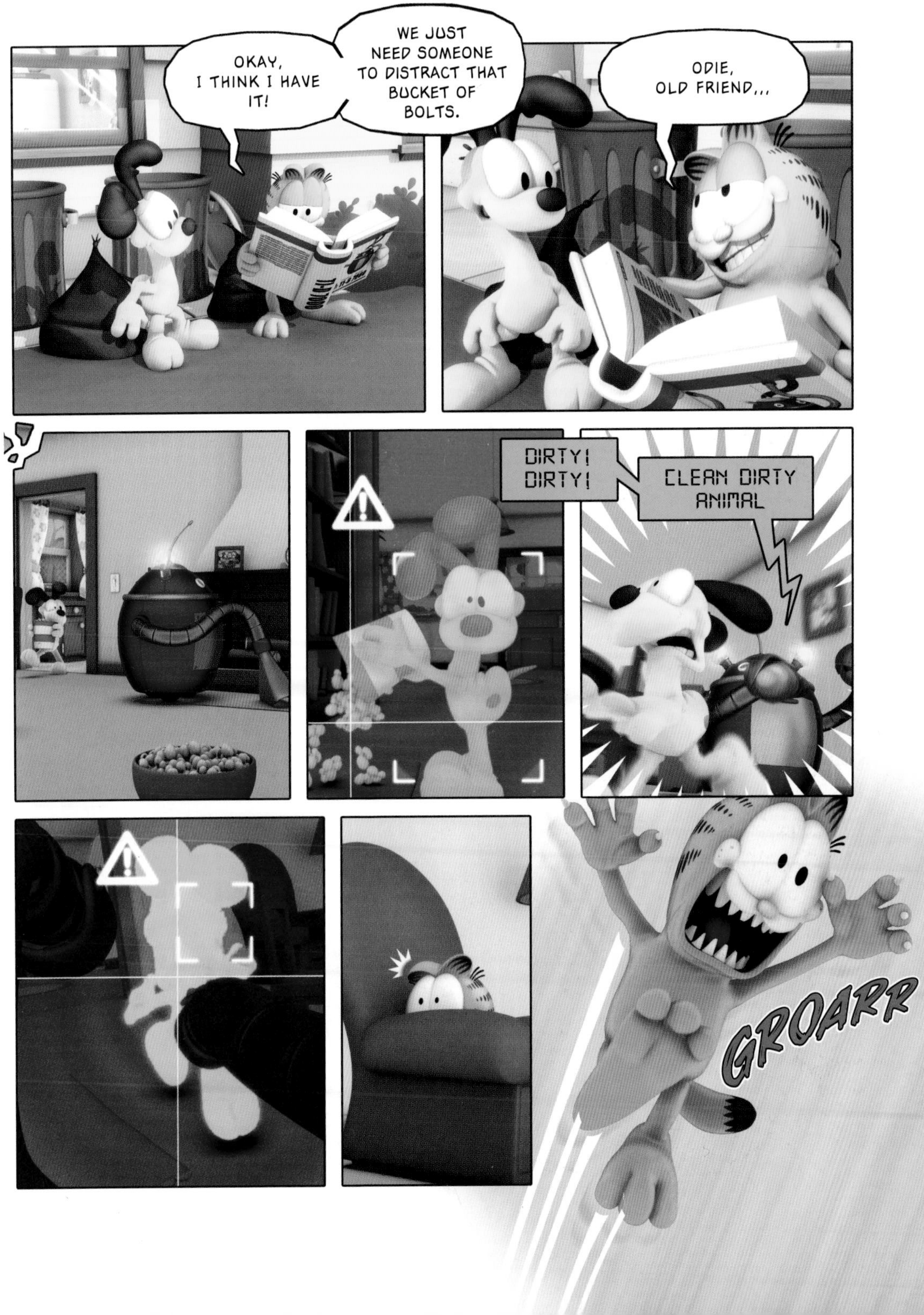

OKAY, I THINK I HAVE IT!
WE JUST NEED SOMEONE TO DISTRACT THAT BUCKET OF BOLTS.
ODIE, OLD FRIEND...
DIRTY! DIRTY!
CLEAN DIRTY ANIMAL
GROARR

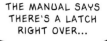

THE MANUAL SAYS THERE'S A LATCH RIGHT OVER...

**WHAM**

DANGER! DANGER!

INTRUDER ALERT

...HERE! AND I'M IN!

**CLIC CLIC CLIC CLIC CLIC**

NOW TO CHANGE THE PROGRAMMING. INSTEAD OF CLEANING UP AFTER PETS...

**CLIC CLIC CLIC**

...IT'S NOW GOING TO CLEAN UP AFTER PET OWNERS.

I DID IT!

**AAAAAAAAAAAAAAAAAAAAAAH**

TARGET ABORTED

⚡ARRGH!⚡ THIS BETTER WORK.

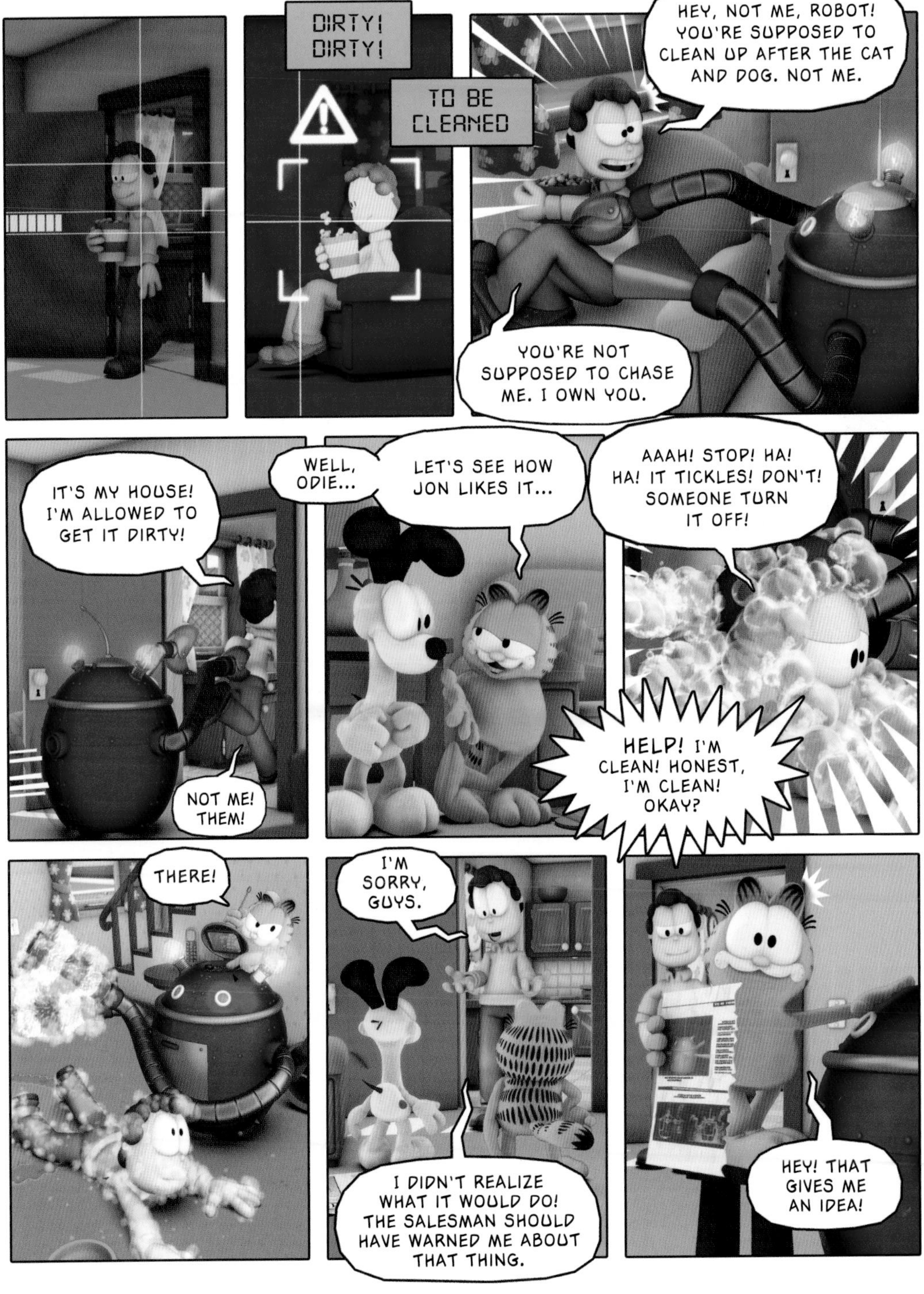
DIRTY! DIRTY!
TO BE CLEANED
HEY, NOT ME, ROBOT! YOU'RE SUPPOSED TO CLEAN UP AFTER THE CAT AND DOG. NOT ME.
YOU'RE NOT SUPPOSED TO CHASE ME. I OWN YOU.
IT'S MY HOUSE! I'M ALLOWED TO GET IT DIRTY!
NOT ME! THEM!
WELL, ODIE...
LET'S SEE HOW JON LIKES IT...
AAAH! STOP! HA! HA! IT TICKLES! DON'T! SOMEONE TURN IT OFF!
HELP! I'M CLEAN! HONEST, I'M CLEAN! OKAY?
THERE!
I'M SORRY, GUYS.
I DIDN'T REALIZE WHAT IT WOULD DO! THE SALESMAN SHOULD HAVE WARNED ME ABOUT THAT THING.
HEY! THAT GIVES ME AN IDEA!

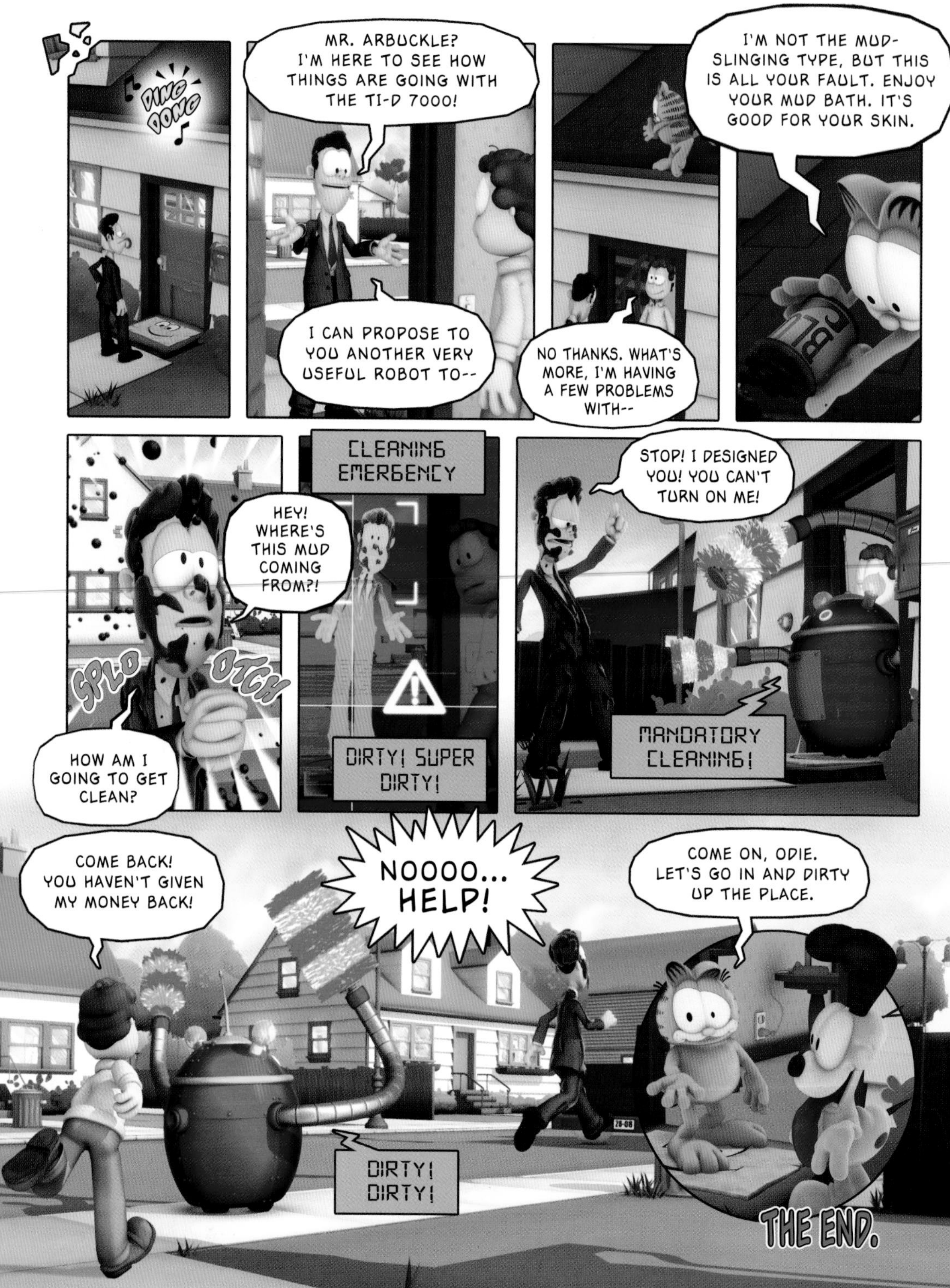
DING DONG
MR. ARBUCKLE? I'M HERE TO SEE HOW THINGS ARE GOING WITH THE TI-D 7000!
I CAN PROPOSE TO YOU ANOTHER VERY USEFUL ROBOT TO--
NO THANKS. WHAT'S MORE, I'M HAVING A FEW PROBLEMS WITH--
I'M NOT THE MUD-SLINGING TYPE, BUT THIS IS ALL YOUR FAULT. ENJOY YOUR MUD BATH. IT'S GOOD FOR YOUR SKIN.
HEY! WHERE'S THIS MUD COMING FROM?!
SPLOOTCH
HOW AM I GOING TO GET CLEAN?
CLEANING EMERGENCY
DIRTY! SUPER DIRTY!
STOP! I DESIGNED YOU! YOU CAN'T TURN ON ME!
MANDATORY CLEANING!
COME BACK! YOU HAVEN'T GIVEN MY MONEY BACK!
NOOOO... HELP!
DIRTY! DIRTY!
COME ON, ODIE. LET'S GO IN AND DIRTY UP THE PLACE.
THE END.

# WATCH OUT FOR PAPERCUTZ™

Question: How are the Papercutz GARFIELD graphic novels physically like Garfield?
Answer: They both keep getting fatter!

Welcome to the fatter-than-ever first THE GARFIELD SHOW graphic novel from Papercutz, the cat-loving people dedicated to publishing great graphic novels for all ages. I'm your forever-dieting, lasagna-loving Editor-in-Chief, Jim Salicrup.

In case you think I'm just joking about our GARFIELD graphic novels getting fatter, just check out how many pages are in this graphic novel. I'll wait. Back so soon? Well, did you notice there's now twice as many pages in the new THE GARFIELD SHOW graphic novel as there were in any single GARFIELD & Co graphic novel? No need to thank me! In fact, if you're a true Garfield fan, I'm not the Jim you care about. That would be this guy:

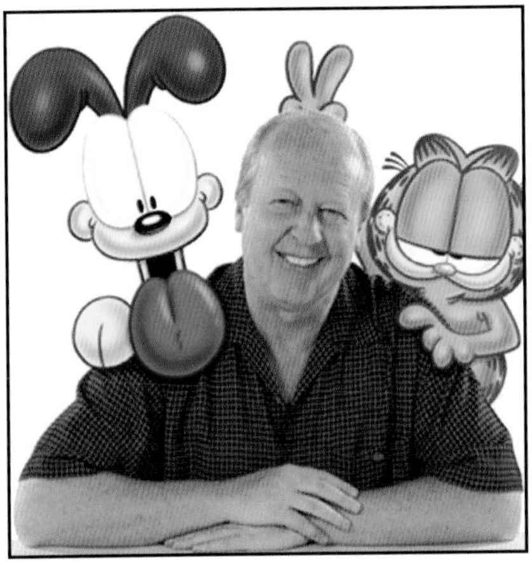

Jim Davis was born July 28, 1945 and was promptly dropped on his head, which would explain his life-long desire to sit around and draw silly pictures. His parents, Jim and Betty Davis, were farmers who raised Black Angus cows and feed crops for the cattle... not to mention 25 cats.

Jim and his little brother, Davey, grew up with a lot of responsibilities and chores, and lots of cats. When Jim was just a little boy he developed asthma — a breathing problem brought on by allergies (probably due to all the hay on the farm). Asthma makes you cough, hack, and wheeze, and Jim had to stay indoors a lot.

One day, when Jim's mom noticed he was bored, she shoved a pencil in his hand and gave him a stack of paper and told him to draw to "keep himself entertained." And he did. One of his first drawings was of a cow. Because it was hardly recognizable, Jim labeled it "cow." Next, he discovered that drawings were funnier if they had words. Before long, Jim had gotten pretty good at drawing. He couldn't stop! He drew on tables. He drew on walls. He even drew on the cattle!

Years later, Jim turned his attention to the comics pages and tried to figure out what was working and why. There were lots of dogs on the comics pages — Snoopy, Marmaduke, Belvedere — but no cats! Jim began sketching cats, drawing on his childhood memories of the 25 farm cats he grew up with. The cat that struck him as the funniest was a big fat grouchy character that he named Garfield after his opinionated grandfather, James Garfield Davis.

Papercutz is super-proud to be publishing THE GARFIELD SHOW, and I can't tell you excited I am that a certain fellow with the initials JD may be at the Papercutz booth at Comic-Con International: San Diego. Look for a complete report in THE GARFIELD SHOW #2 "Jon's Night Out." Until then, be sure to keep your lasagna in a safe place!

Thanks,

Jim

**STAY IN TOUCH!**

| | |
|---|---|
| EMAIL: | SALICRUP@PAPERCUTZ.COM |
| WEB: | WWW.PAPERCUTZ.COM |
| TWITTER: | @PAPERCUTZGN |
| FACEBOOK: | PAPERCUTZGRAPHICNOVELS |
| BIRTHDAY CARDS: | PAPERCUTZ, 160 BROADWAY, SUITE 700, EAST WING, NEW YORK, NY 10038 |

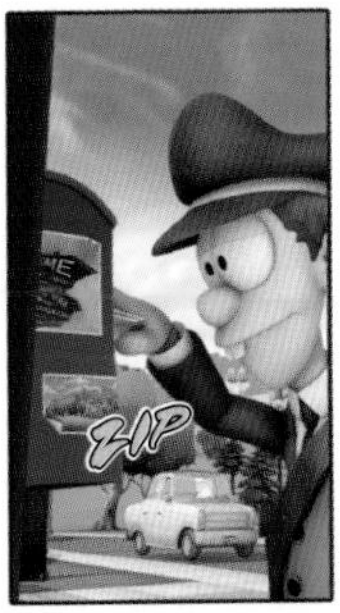
ZIP

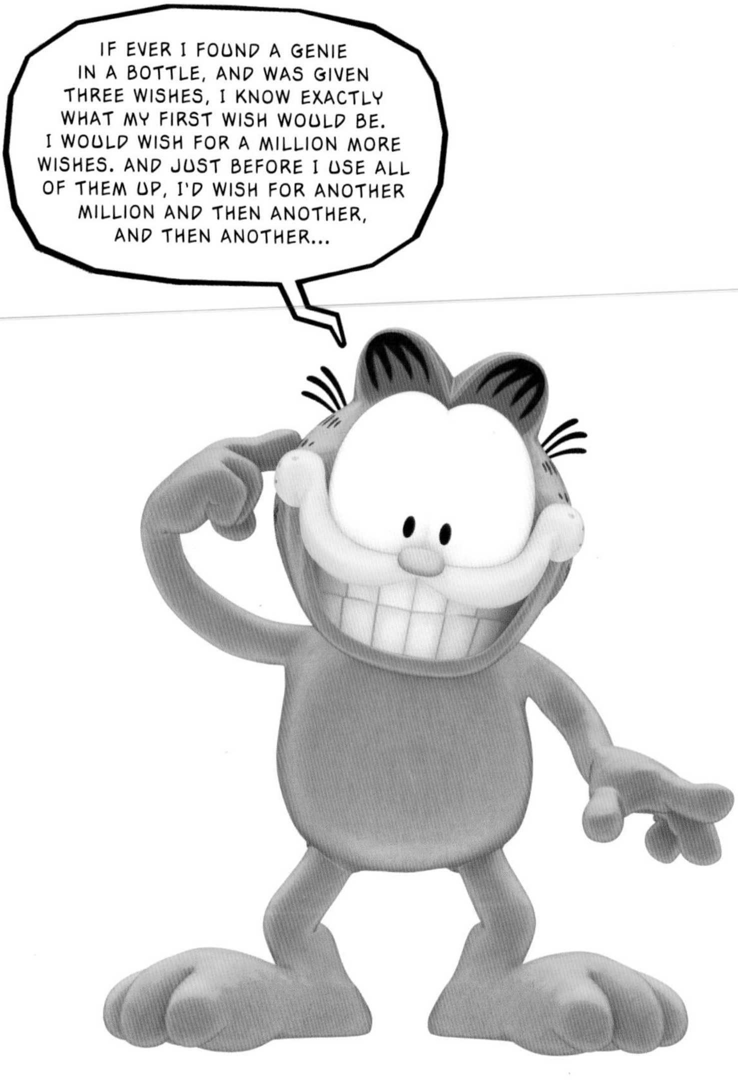
IF EVER I FOUND A GENIE IN A BOTTLE, AND WAS GIVEN THREE WISHES, I KNOW EXACTLY WHAT MY FIRST WISH WOULD BE. I WOULD WISH FOR A MILLION MORE WISHES. AND JUST BEFORE I USE ALL OF THEM UP, I'D WISH FOR ANOTHER MILLION AND THEN ANOTHER, AND THEN ANOTHER...

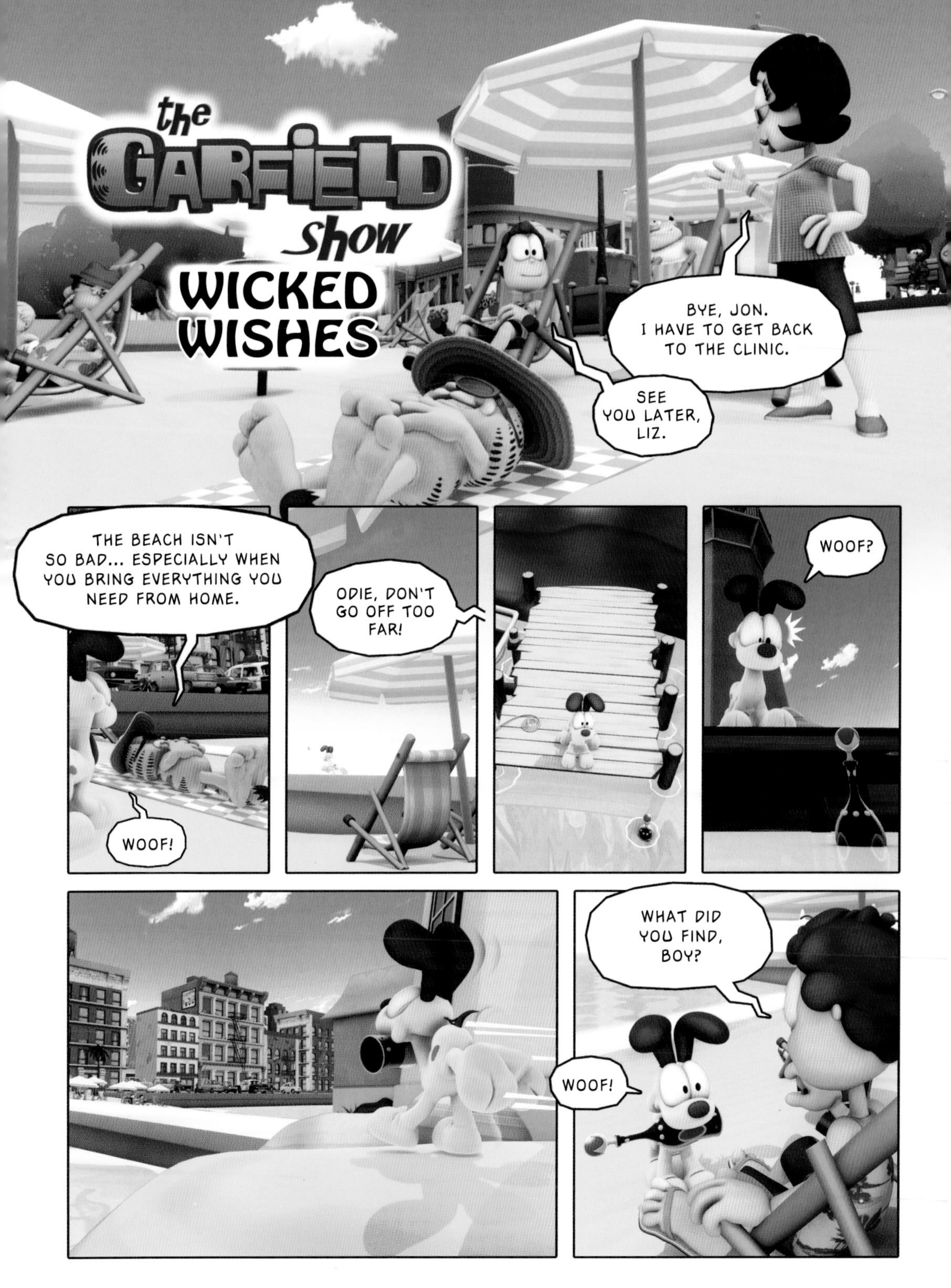
the GARFIELD show
WICKED WISHES
BYE, JON. I HAVE TO GET BACK TO THE CLINIC.
SEE YOU LATER, LIZ.
THE BEACH ISN'T SO BAD... ESPECIALLY WHEN YOU BRING EVERYTHING YOU NEED FROM HOME.
WOOF!
ODIE, DON'T GO OFF TOO FAR!
WOOF?
WHAT DID YOU FIND, BOY?
WOOF!

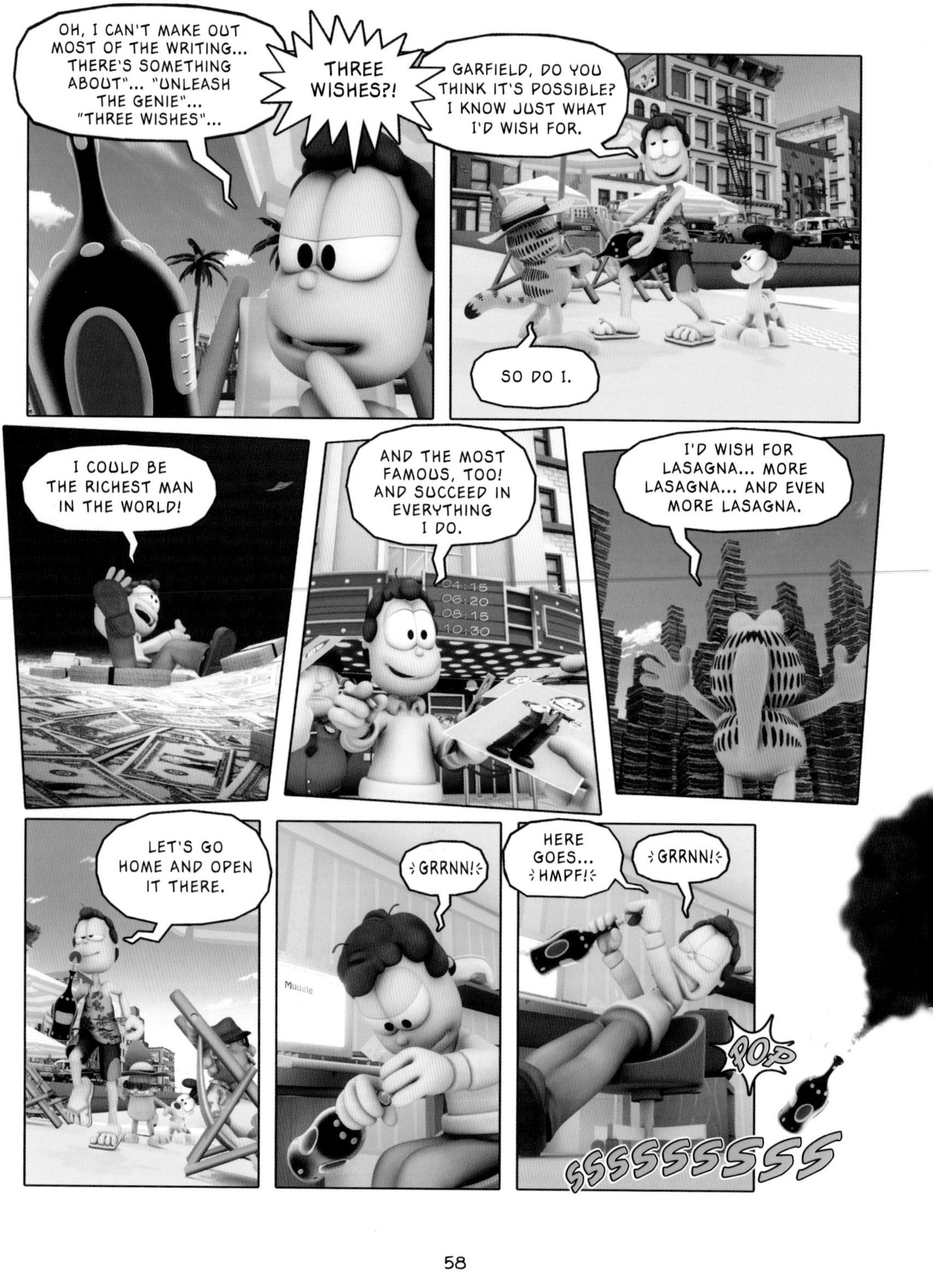
OH, I CAN'T MAKE OUT MOST OF THE WRITING... THERE'S SOMETHING ABOUT"... "UNLEASH THE GENIE"... "THREE WISHES"...
THREE WISHES?!
GARFIELD, DO YOU THINK IT'S POSSIBLE? I KNOW JUST WHAT I'D WISH FOR.
SO DO I.
I COULD BE THE RICHEST MAN IN THE WORLD!
AND THE MOST FAMOUS, TOO! AND SUCCEED IN EVERYTHING I DO.
04:15
06:20
08:15
10:30
I'D WISH FOR LASAGNA... MORE LASAGNA... AND EVEN MORE LASAGNA.
LET'S GO HOME AND OPEN IT THERE.
GRRNN!
HERE GOES... HMPF!
GRRNN!
POP
SSSSSSSSSS

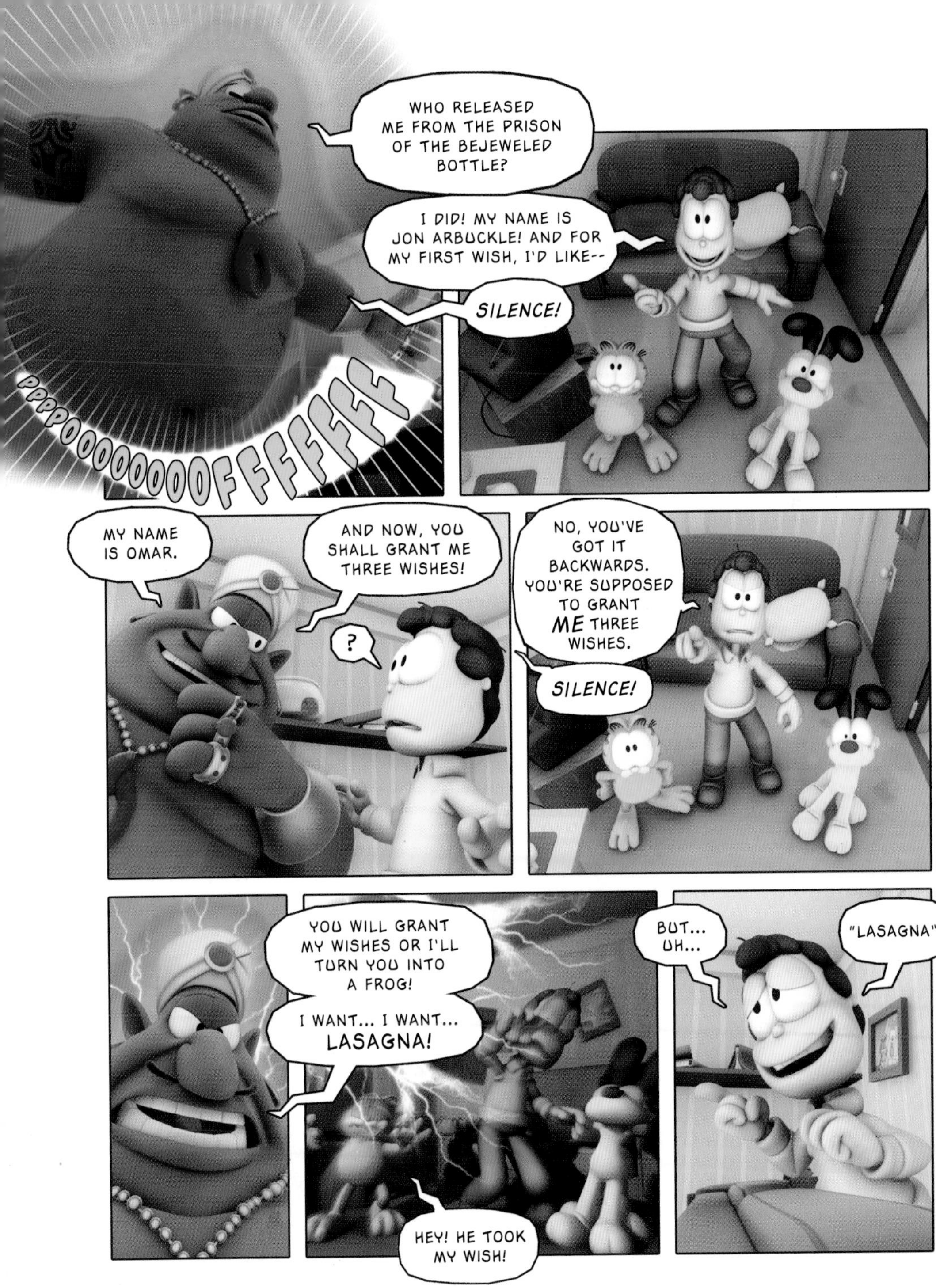
WHO RELEASED ME FROM THE PRISON OF THE BEJEWELED BOTTLE?
I DID! MY NAME IS JON ARBUCKLE! AND FOR MY FIRST WISH, I'D LIKE--
SILENCE!
PPPPOOOOOOOOOFFFFFFF
MY NAME IS OMAR.
AND NOW, YOU SHALL GRANT ME THREE WISHES!
?
NO, YOU'VE GOT IT BACKWARDS. YOU'RE SUPPOSED TO GRANT ME THREE WISHES.
SILENCE!
YOU WILL GRANT MY WISHES OR I'LL TURN YOU INTO A FROG!
I WANT... I WANT... LASAGNA!
HEY! HE TOOK MY WISH!
BUT... UH...
"LASAGNA"?

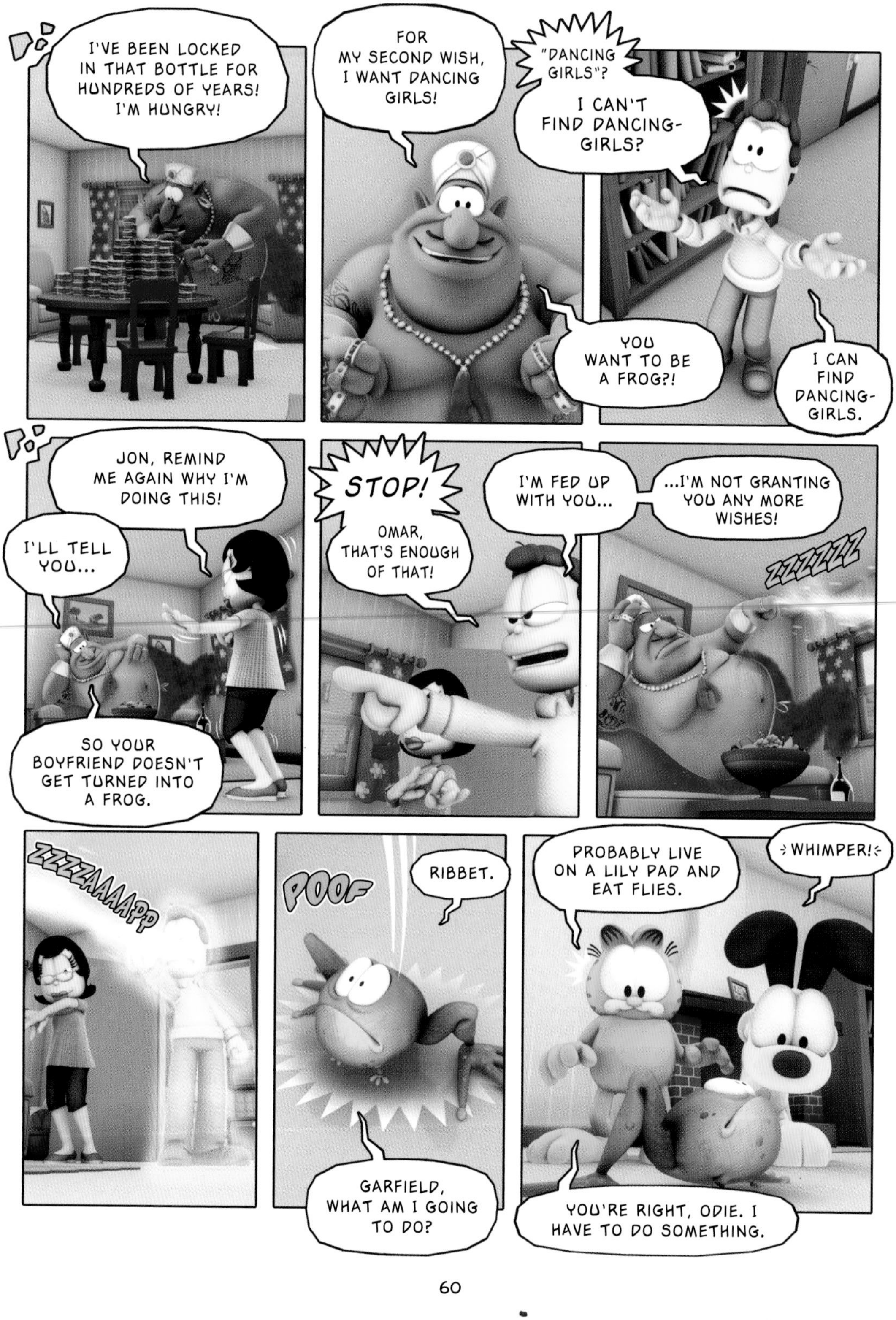

I'VE BEEN LOCKED IN THAT BOTTLE FOR HUNDREDS OF YEARS! I'M HUNGRY!
FOR MY SECOND WISH, I WANT DANCING GIRLS!
"DANCING GIRLS"?
I CAN'T FIND DANCING-GIRLS?
YOU WANT TO BE A FROG?!
I CAN FIND DANCING-GIRLS.
JON, REMIND ME AGAIN WHY I'M DOING THIS!
I'LL TELL YOU...
SO YOUR BOYFRIEND DOESN'T GET TURNED INTO A FROG.
STOP!
OMAR, THAT'S ENOUGH OF THAT!
I'M FED UP WITH YOU...
...I'M NOT GRANTING YOU ANY MORE WISHES!
ZZZZZZZ
ZZZZZAAAAPP
POOF
RIBBET.
GARFIELD, WHAT AM I GOING TO DO?
PROBABLY LIVE ON A LILY PAD AND EAT FLIES.
WHIMPER!
YOU'RE RIGHT, ODIE. I HAVE TO DO SOMETHING.

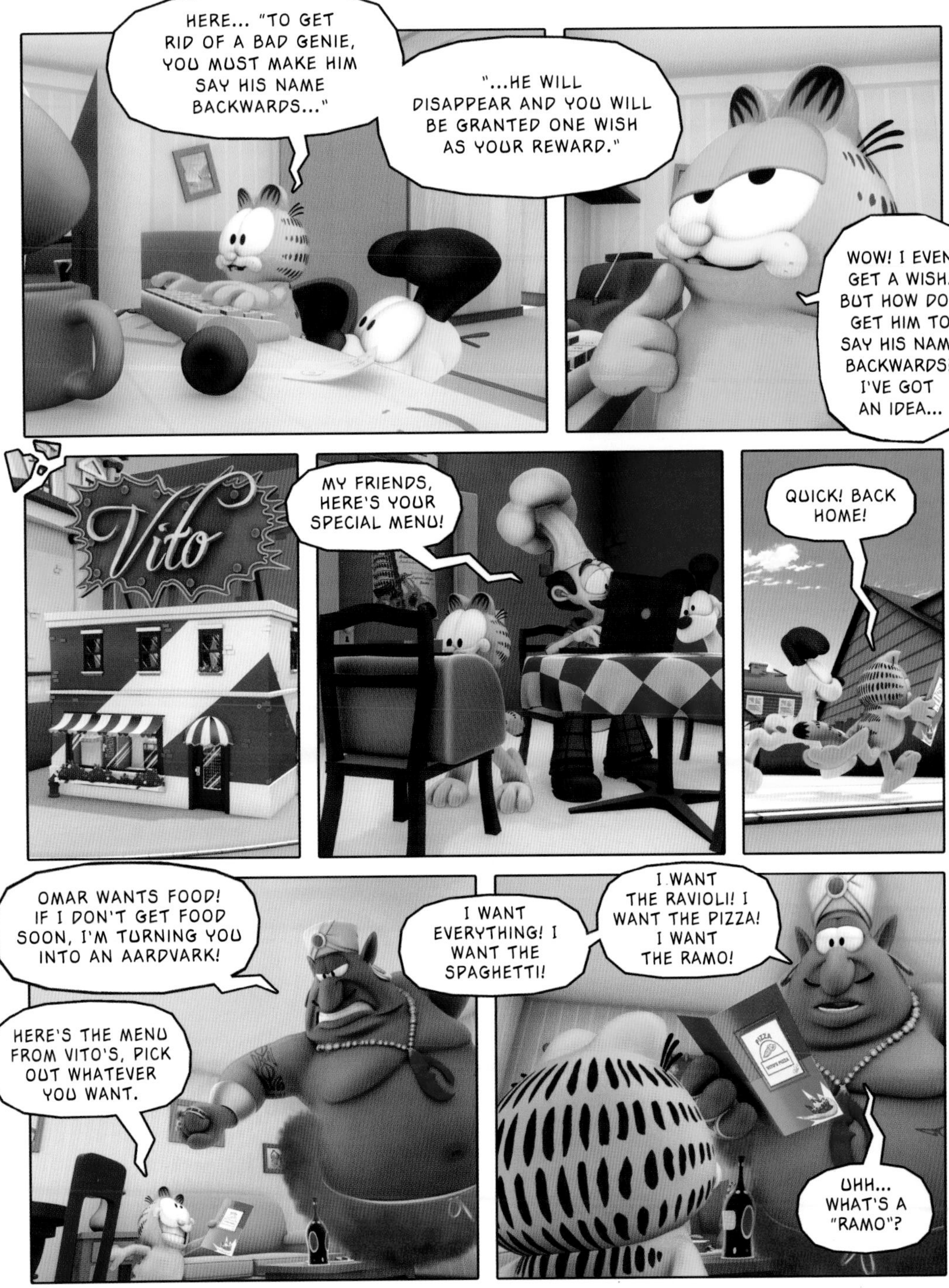
HERE... "TO GET RID OF A BAD GENIE, YOU MUST MAKE HIM SAY HIS NAME BACKWARDS..."
"...HE WILL DISAPPEAR AND YOU WILL BE GRANTED ONE WISH AS YOUR REWARD."
WOW! I EVEN GET A WISH. BUT HOW DO I GET HIM TO SAY HIS NAME BACKWARDS? I'VE GOT AN IDEA...
Vito
MY FRIENDS, HERE'S YOUR SPECIAL MENU!
QUICK! BACK HOME!
OMAR WANTS FOOD! IF I DON'T GET FOOD SOON, I'M TURNING YOU INTO AN AARDVARK!
HERE'S THE MENU FROM VITO'S, PICK OUT WHATEVER YOU WANT.
I WANT EVERYTHING! I WANT THE SPAGHETTI!
I WANT THE RAVIOLI! I WANT THE PIZZA! I WANT THE RAMO!
UHH... WHAT'S A "RAMO"?

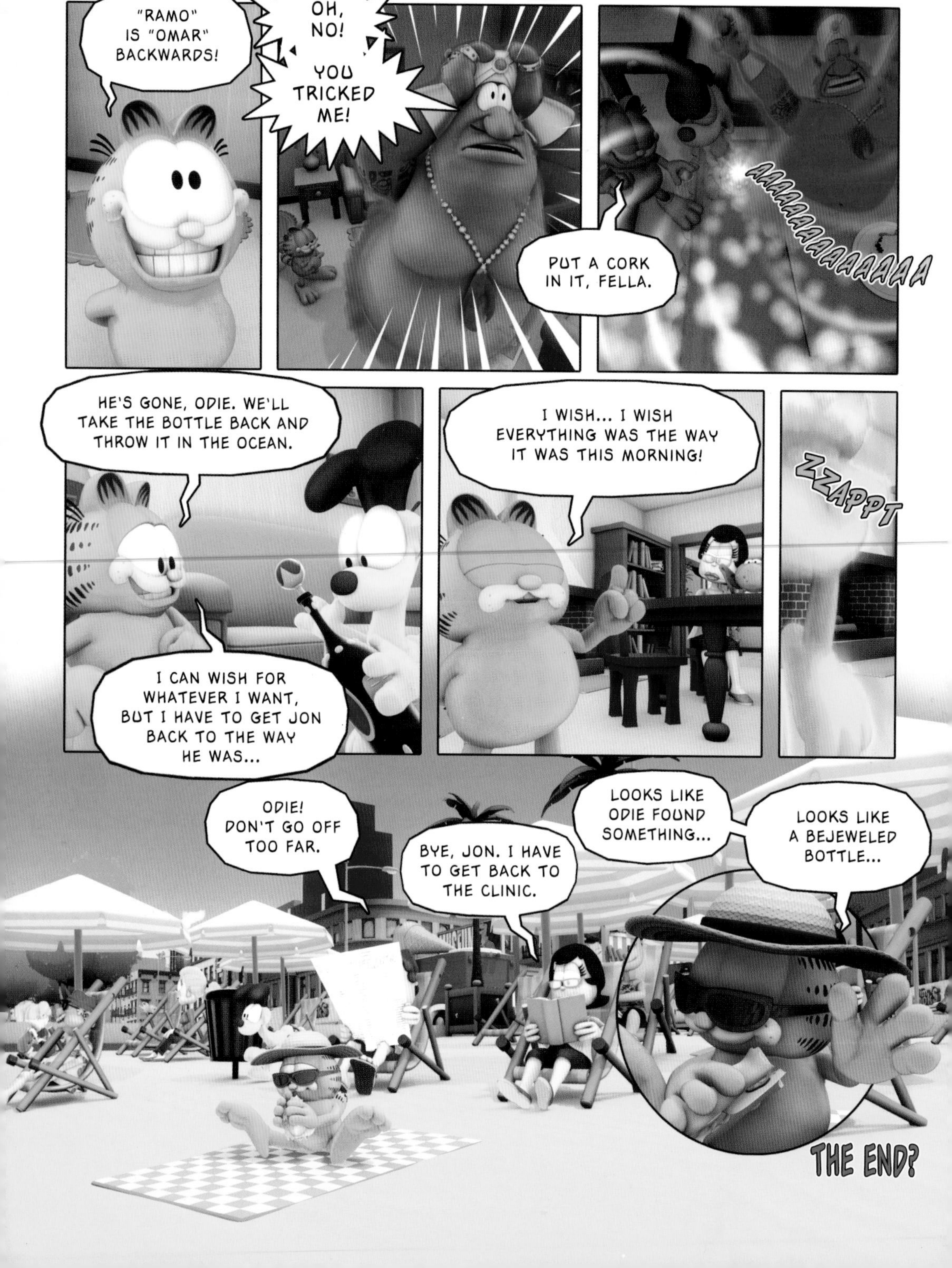
"RAMO" IS "OMAR" BACKWARDS!
OH, NO!
YOU TRICKED ME!
AAAAAAAAAAAAAAAA
PUT A CORK IN IT, FELLA.
HE'S GONE, ODIE. WE'LL TAKE THE BOTTLE BACK AND THROW IT IN THE OCEAN.
I CAN WISH FOR WHATEVER I WANT, BUT I HAVE TO GET JON BACK TO THE WAY HE WAS...
I WISH... I WISH EVERYTHING WAS THE WAY IT WAS THIS MORNING!
ZZAPPT
ODIE! DON'T GO OFF TOO FAR.
BYE, JON. I HAVE TO GET BACK TO THE CLINIC.
LOOKS LIKE ODIE FOUND SOMETHING...
LOOKS LIKE A BEJEWELED BOTTLE...
THE END?

# PAPERCATZ ™

WE KEEP TELLING YOU HOW MUCH WE LOVE CATS HERE AT PAPERCUTZ, SO WE THOUGHT WE'D RUN A FEW PICS OF OUR CATS AS PROOF POSITIVE!

WHILE PAPERCUTZ PRODUCTION COORDINATOR BETH SCORZATO CAN BOSS AROUND EVRYONE IN THE OFFICE, WE BET WHEN SHE GOES HOME, THE REAL BOSS IS HER CAT, "AKIMA."

HERE'S THE GARFIELD SHOW'S EDITOR MICHAEL PETRANEK'S CRIME-FIGHTING CAT, "ROBIN." TOGETHER, MICHAEL AND ROBIN ARE QUITE A DYNAMIC DUO!

HELPING HIM ON THE PRODUCTION OF OUR CLASSICS ILLUSTRATED GRAPHIC NOVELS ARE ORTHO'S CATS "LUNA" AND "CHLOE." OR DOES ORTHO ACTUALLY HELP THEM PUT IT ALL TOGETHER?

WHEN LOOKING FOR INSPIRATION ON HOW TO CREATE MORE ATTENTION FOR THE GARFIELD SHOW, PAPERCUTZ MARKETING DIRECTOR JESSE POST WILL OFTEN CONSULT HIS CATS "RUDIE" AND "JANGO."

PAPERCUTZ EDITOR-IN-CHIEF JIM SALICRUP GOT HIS CAT, "AZRAEL," AS A RESCUE. AZRAEL'S FORMER OWNER WAS REALLY A NASTY CHARACTER!

EDITOR MICHAEL PETRANEK'S FAMILY DOG, ZEUS, IS NOT A CAT AND DOES NOT BELONG HERE. BUT, HE KIND OF LOOKS LIKE ODIE, SO WE'LL LET THIS ONE SLIDE...

 © Peyo - 2013 - Licensed through Lafig Belgium - www.smurf.com

# More Great Graphic Novels from PAPERCUTZ™

FULL COLOR GRAPHIC NOVEL BASED ON THE DVD!
TinkerBell and the Lost Treasure
PAPERCUTZ

**DISNEY FAIRIES #12**
**"Tinker Bell and the Lost Treasure"**
Tink must save Pixie Hollow in this story based on the hit DVD!

Guillaume Bianco
Antonello Dalena
Ernest & Rebecca

**ERNEST & REBECCA #4**
**"The Land of Walking Stones"**
A 6 ½ year old girl and her microbial buddy against the world!

Béka and Crip
Dance Class
To Russia, With Love
PAPERCUTZ


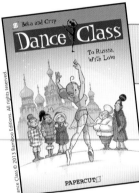

**DANCE CLASS #5**
**"To Russia, with Love"**
The girls travel to Russia to perform "The Nutcracker"!

Monster Turkey
PAPERCUTZ

**MONSTER #4**
**"Monster Turkey"**
The almost normal adventures of an almost ordinary family... with a pet monster!

THE SMURFLINGS
PAPERCUTZ

**THE SMURFS #15**
**"The Smurflings"**
Are the Smurfs getting... younger?

SYBIL
the Backpack Fairy
"Princess Nina"


**SYBIL THE BACKPACK FAIRY #4**
**"Princess Nina"**
Sybil and Nina's excellent adventure through time!

Available at better booksellers everywhere!

Or order directly from us! DISNEY FAIRIES is available in paperback for $7.99, in hardcover for $11.99; ERNEST & REBECCA is $11.99 in hardcover only; DANCE CLASS is available in hardcover only for $11.99; MONSTER is available in hardcover only for $9.99; THE SMURFS are available in paperback for $5.99, in hardcover for $10.99; and SYBIL THE BACKPACK FAIRY is available in hardcover only for $11.99.

Please add $4.00 for postage and handling for the first book, add $1.00 for each additional book.
Please make check payable to NBM Publishing. Send to: PAPERCUTZ,160 Broadway, Suite 700, East Wing, New York, NY 10038 (1-800-886-1223) or order online at papercutz.com

# DATE DUE

| | | | |
|---|---|---|---|
| | | | |
| | | | |
| | | | |
| | | | |
| | | | |
| | | | |
| | | | |
| | | | |
| | | | |
| | | | |
| | | | |
| | | | |
| | | | |
| | | | |
| | | | |
| | | | |
| | | | |
| | | | PRINTED IN U.S.A. |